"So you think we should take the plunge and get married?"

Jeb asked sarcastically. "You'll be my barefooted fishwife and I'll be your redneck lover—"

"Don't!" she cried. "You're *not* a redneck good ol' boy, Jeb Albright."

"And I wonder if you have any genuine idea what you're offering...or what you'd be getting." He bent, and before she knew what was happening, Jeb had swung her into his arms in one effortless movement. "You need to know exactly what you're getting. Exactly." At the base of her throat he slid a finger under the strand of pearls nestled there. Lower he went, as he trailed his fingertips through the valley between her breasts. His hands drifted lower still....

Mariah moaned softly as she surged against him in silent invitation. *Yes*, she thought. He was made of the stuff that endured and lasted a lifetime. And this was what she needed, more than life.

Dear Reader,

In 1993 beloved, bestselling author Diana Palmer launched the FABULOUS FATHERS series with *Emmett* (SR#910), which was her 50th Silhouette book. Readers fell in love with that Long, Tall Texan who discovered the meaning of love and fatherhood, and ever since, the FABULOUS FATHERS series has been a favorite. And now, to celebrate the publication of the *50th* FABULOUS FATHERS book, Silhouette Romance is very proud to present a brand-new novel by Diana Palmer, *Mystery Man*, and Fabulous Father Canton Rourke.

Silhouette Romance is just chock-full of special books this month! We've got *Miss Maxwell Becomes a Mom,* book one of Donna Clayton's new miniseries, THE SINGLE DADDY CLUB. And Alice Sharpe's *Missing: One Bride* is book one of our SURPRISE BRIDES trio, three irresistible books by three wonderful authors about very unusual wedding situations.

Rounding out the month is Jodi O'Donnell's newest title, *Real Marriage Material,* in which a sexy man of the land gets tamed. Robin Wells's *Husband and Wife...Again* tells the tale of a divorced couple reuniting in a delightful way. And finally, in *Daddy for Hire* by Joey Light, a hunk of a man becomes the most muscular nanny there ever was, all for love of his little girl.

Enjoy Diana Palmer's *Mystery Man* and all of our wonderful books this month. There's just no better way to start off springtime than with six books bursting with love!

Regards,

Melissa Senate
Senior Editor
Silhouette Books

Please address questions and book requests to:
Silhouette Reader Service
U.S.: 3010 Walden Ave., P.O. Box 1325, Buffalo, NY 14269
Canadian: P.O. Box 609, Fort Erie, Ont. L2A 5X3

REAL MARRIAGE MATERIAL

MATERIAL

Jodi O'Donnell

Silhouette
R O M A N C E™
Published by Silhouette Books
America's Publisher of Contemporary Romance

ACKNOWLEDGMENTS:

My thanks to Don Anderson, owner of Don's Guide Service on
Lake Texoma, for keeping me straight on striper fishing, and to
Larry Martin, for filling me in on adoption procedures in Texas.
My thanks also to Alyson Brown for keeping me legal. Any
errors concerning these areas are entirely my fault.

DEDICATION:

For my agent, Pam Hopkins—the real deal, the genuine article,
the best!

 SILHOUETTE BOOKS

ISBN 0-373-19213-4

REAL MARRIAGE MATERIAL

Books by Jodi O'Donnell

Silhouette Romance

Still Sweet on Him #969
The Farmer Takes a Wife #992
A Man To Remember #1021
Daddy Was a Cowboy #1080
Real Marriage Material #1213

Silhouette Special Edition

Of Texas Ladies, Cowboys...and Babies #1045

JODI O'DONNELL

grew up one of fourteen children in small-town Iowa. As a result, she loves to explore in her writing how family relationships influence who and why we love as we do.

Jodi is a two-time National Readers' Choice Finalist and winner of Romance Writers of America's Golden Heart Award. She's married to the hometown boy she has known since fifth grade and lives near Dallas in a ninety-five-year-old Victorian home with her husband, Darrel, and two dogs, Rio and Leia.

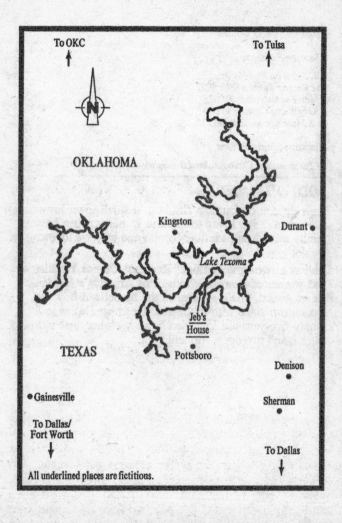

To OKC

To Tulsa

N

OKLAHOMA

Kingston

Durant

Lake Texoma

Jeb's
House

TEXAS

Pottsboro

Denison

Gainesville

Sherman

To Dallas/
Fort Worth

To Dallas

All underlined places are fictitious.

Chapter One

How positively...uncivilized, Mariah Duncan decided as she followed the directions that took her out of Sherman and into the brushy country surrounding Lake Texoma. Wildflowers of every color rioted along the roadside, rousing banners for a bright new season that dressed up the overgrown bracken behind them.

It had always intrigued her that one could leave any metropolitan area in Texas and within minutes be virtually in the wild. Not that Texoma was inordinately remote. Still, it occurred to her that, should she take Wiley Albright on as a client, she'd be making this rather rugged journey regularly.

Spying a landmark, Mariah braked gently, tires bumping over the patched asphalt. Now came the tricky part, following the kind of instructions true locals gave. "Keep on a-goin' till you pass the picnic area on your right," Mr. Albright had told her. "There's a gravel road just beyond, but don't take it, just slow down a bit, 'cause there's a hump comin' up that'll put your stomach up 'round your tonsils if you ain't lookin' for it. Then I'd say maybe a mile, mile and a quarter farther, you'll see a sign for Bubba J.'s Everything For Fishing And Camping. Can't miss it. Turn left past Bubba J.'s and take the lane behind the store on down the hill. The house there—that's the place.''

And so it was. The house sitting among a stand of pecan trees was actually an older-model mobile home. A skirt of flashing rimmed the bottom in the same beige as the trailer's siding. Upon the attached porch, its floor and steps covered in green artificial turf, sat a well-used barbecue and a couple of blue-and-white-webbed lawn chairs. Past the mobile home, the lane continued down to the shore of the lake, where there was a private boat ramp and both a small boat house and a U-shaped dock. Incongruous with the rest of the modest surroundings, a sleek and expensive-looking boat, secured in the narrow slip formed by the dock, bobbed in the water under the shade of a weeping willow.

The whole effect was placid and prosaic—and a world away from what she was used to. She had yet to learn exactly what service Mr. Albright required of her, and she had to admit she was stumped. Most of her clients lived the hectic lives of city dwellers—hence their appreciation for the enrichment her services brought them.

Mariah parked on the shady side of the trailer, next to the huge satellite dish she presumed to be de rigueur in rural areas, and gathered her bulky organizer into her arms. Leaving her car, she climbed the stairs to the porch and knocked firmly on the frame of the screen door, with no answer.

Becoming concerned for the first time, she checked her watch. Mr. Albright had said after six. And this had to be the right place. Hugging the black leather organizer to her chest—typical of spring, the day's warmth was dispelling rapidly with sunset—Mariah glanced around the yard and thought yet again how truly wild this setting was.

A whole different kind of person lived in this environment, she mused, descending the steps slowly. People who had their own ideas about what constituted a civilized lifestyle—which was often protected by means of Smith & Wesson.

Had she been naive coming out here merely on the basis of a friendly phone call?

Nonsense, Mariah told herself staunchly. Still, she decided to err on the side of caution. She would drive back up the lane to the store on the corner and wait there. Although Mr. Albright hadn't mentioned Bubba J.'s other than as a landmark, the proximity of the business to the house—plus the well-traveled path leading from its back door to the trailer—led her to guess an association existed between the two.

She was halfway to her car when she heard a sound coming from the direction of the dock. With a private nod of confirmation, she rounded the corner of the mobile home just as a tall man did the same.

They collided, and she had the impression of a broad, unyielding chest pressed against hers before callused hands grasped both her upper arms. Whether the hands were meant to steady or constrain wasn't immediately obvious. What *was* clear was the physical impact of this man, solid and real.

Her chin came up, and she was blinded by the setting sun behind the man's shoulder. The man's physical presence and the setting sun, plus the realization that a barking dog was insinuating itself between them, caused her survival instincts to go into overdrive. Oh, she *had* been naive!

Mariah dropped her organizer in order to flatten her hands against that firm expanse of muscle and shove herself away. An ant might as well have tried to move a mountain.

Now totally unnerved, she struggled madly. "Let me go!"

"Whatever you say," came the surprisingly mild answer, and suddenly Mariah found herself without support and backpedaling for footing on the muddy ground. Arms flailing, she nearly fell, catching her balance only at the last second. Then she almost lost her footing again as the dog doused her and the man in a spray of water as it shook itself.

"Lucy!" He bent slightly to loop his fingers under the dog's collar and retreated a few feet. She understood the precaution as the animal strained against the restriction before she, too, dropped back. The dog, a white one with black markings of indeterminate breed, sat on her haunches and leaned against the man's leg.

It was then Mariah noticed the dog's tongue lolling in a grin of barely contained welcome. So this was the vicious beast that had sent her into a near-frenzy.

"You almost scared me to death, Mr. Albright," she explained crossly. More from embarrassment than necessity, Mariah concentrated on brushing her clothes off.

"Did I, now?" he drawled in a tone that said he wasn't quite sorry. It brought back all of her apprehension. Where was the affable man she'd talked with on the phone?

"You are Mr. Albright, aren't you?" she asked with a boldness she hardly felt. She couldn't prevent herself, however, from raising one hand to finger the strand of pearls at her throat in an ingrained gesture of security, as if to reassure herself after the fright he'd given her—and still was rousing in her, for she watched his mouth tighten visibly at her action.

He stooped to retrieve her organizer, wiping it against the thigh of his jeans before handing it to her.

"Yes," he finally answered her question. The word was cautious, which puzzled her. She was the one on unfamiliar territory right now. The one who had something to be wary of, something to lose.

His face now visible to her, she studied it, looking for clues. What she discerned first was that he was younger than she'd believed, judging from his voice over the telephone. She could see why he himself had been unperturbed by Lucy's dousing: the faded white T-shirt he wore, patchy with sweat and stains and even a hole or two, looked in little danger of being damaged by a few drops of water off a dog. In fact, his tousled, dark brown hair was already wet, as if sometime in the past half hour he'd dunked his head to cool off and hadn't even bothered to finger-comb away any residual moisture.

Yes, he looked wild and uncivilized—and not a little annoyed with her, for some reason.

How was she to get past this unfortunate start with this man? Or perhaps the question was, did she really want to?

"You did say between six and six-thirty," Mariah said, unable to keep the defensiveness from her voice,

His eyebrows rose. "I did?" Another of those cautious, unrevealing questions.

Now *she* became vexed. She firmly agreed with the motto that the customer was always right, but intimating she might have made a mistake in date or time cast doubt upon her care for detail, which was one of the main benefits she claimed she would provide her clients.

"I have my notes on your phone call to set up the appointment and the directions you gave me right here," she said crisply as she opened the organizer to her calendar. Her actions were stayed by a raised hand.

"I think I know what's happened," he said, features relaxing a little. He nodded in the direction of Bubba J.'s at the top of the hill. "You must be looking for my uncle."

Mariah shook her head. "You're not Wiley Albright?"

"I'm Jeb Albright, Wiley's nephew."

"Oh! Yes, he did mention you." And she had forgotten, mostly because she'd gotten the impression this meeting had to do with a youngster rather than an adult. Mariah had to smile at the mix-up even if she was still puzzled as to why her showing up unexpectedly would provoke such wariness in this man. Unless that was the usual state of affairs with Jeb Albright. "And am I right in assuming he didn't mention me to you?" she asked.

"Seems that way, doesn't it?" He actually returned her smile with a half smile of his own, revealing a thumbnail-sized dimple in his cheek.

The sight of that dimple did wonders for his looks—and something to her respiration rate.

She was compelled to try another smile on him. "No telling what must have gone through your mind when this woman showed up without warning..."

He dropped his chin to rub it, slanting her a suddenly probing look from under his lashes. "I'm not sure what I thought, ma'am," he murmured in a not altogether unappealing backwoods twang, his voice at a pitch that could have been pensive or provocative. Either way, it sent a shiver down Mariah's spine.

It was just another chill from the now-brisk afternoon, she told herself as she fell back into her formal persona. "Well, then, proper introductions are in order. I'm Mariah Duncan," she said, extending her hand. "From Saved by the..."

Her voice trailed off as she saw Jeb stare at her hand. His own curled closed at his side. What now? she thought as the dog stretched inquiringly toward her fingers.

"Lucy, no," he commanded. "We've already done enough damage."

The dog drew obediently back.

"She doesn't look bent on harm." Her hand still extended, Mariah added rather pointedly, "Neither am I." But she felt somehow the assurance was needed.

His gaze cut to hers, again probing. He hesitated before explaining stiffly, "It's just that we're neither of us too savory right now, ma'am."

"I see." Now that he mentioned it, she did detect what smelled like a combination of silty lake water, honest perspiration and wet fur, which was actually not all that unpleasant, especially out here in the fresh air. Mariah might have told him so except for his wariness, which left her feeling even more self-conscious.

On another impulse, she crouched, hand still extended, and said softly, "Lucy, is it?"

The direct greeting was more than the dog could stand. Feathery tail slashing back and forth like a windshield wiper, the animal shoved her nose into Mariah's palm and gave a hearty sniff before moving in to try for more-intimate contact, namely Mariah's face. She managed to avoid the invasive advances of Lucy's questing nose while giving the dog a few friendly pats.

Up close, Lucy's odor *was* a little overpowering, but Mariah bore up as best she could, since she could see from the corner of her eye the softening of Jeb's features she'd hoped for. Not that she'd exactly been trying to soothe the savage beast. Still, Mariah discovered she'd achieved her aim when she turned her face upward and found herself the recipient of another one of those grudging half smiles—as if his mouth was unused to tipping up at the corners—that seemed to suggest he appreciated the spirit of her gesture.

Her heart quickened in response. For the first time, she saw how handsome Jeb Albright was—or might be, once he'd had the chance to tidy up. Although it was only April, his strong features were tanned. His hair could have used a good trimming, even if the way it hung over his forehead had its allure. Beneath the dusting of a five-o'clock shadow, his jaw and chin and mouth were finely formed. Her gaze wandering, she noticed that the worn-out T-shirt that had first caught her attention covered—quite snugly—wide shoulders and the defined musculature of the chest she'd been fleetingly pressed against. From her position crouched at his feet, she could see up close that his jeans, like his T-shirt, were worn, stained—and fit just as well.

He looked wild, all right. Wild and…real.

Mariah glanced up to find dark-lashed blue eyes perusing

her as thoroughly. Abruptly she was certain she must have imagined both his wariness and his regard, for his gaze was filled with some earthy, predatory emotion. And rather than holding her at bay, it pulled her to him, kindling in her an answering primitiveness.

She'd heard the phrase *animal magnetism* before, but this was the first time she'd experienced it in the flesh, so to speak.

Another wave of fear washed over her, this one out of concern for her emotional well-being rather than her physical safety. Yes, she could see the seduction in that earthiness, how it could become a demanding need.

Of course, that had been the accusation Stephen had thrown at her before she left him—just as he'd also told her a woman like her could never understand such a need.

Escaping those thoughts, she lit upon the first subject that came to mind. "So you must be the *J* in Bubba J.'s."

At her statement, Jeb's expression clouded over yet again. "Nope," he said curtly.

"Well, I just wondered." Her fingers groped for the pearls. "A lot of boys in Texas grow up being called that—"

"There is no Bubba J.," he interrupted, then with the same stiffness he'd shown before, he went on, "It's supposed to give the feeling of us being 'just folks.' You know, what city people expect to find when they come out here—" He cut off his explanation with a sound of impatience. "It's just a name. That's all."

"Fine." Quite obviously she'd hit a sore spot. Several, in fact. This, along with the hazard to her emotional equilibrium she'd just experienced, led Mariah to decide she might be best to conclude this interview, such as it had been, and return to Sherman, even if she still had no idea why she'd been called here. Now, though, she really wasn't sure she wanted to know.

But before she could act on that decision, she heard a

door open and close distantly behind her. Rising, Mariah saw the man who must be the real Wiley Albright hurrying toward her and Jeb from Bubba J.'s.

"I'm late, I'm late, I know I am," he called to them, pointing his hands skyward, stick-up style. "I was teachin' Robbie how to close up and clean forgot the time."

"Everything okay?" Jeb asked Wiley.

"Fine, son, just fine," Wiley assured him as he came to a stop in front of them both, Lucy panting at his feet as she waited with scarcely restrained excitement to deliver her end-of-the-day welcome.

"Mariah Duncan, Mr. Albright," Mariah volunteered formally. This time she didn't offer her hand, hoping to avoid another awkward moment and to extract herself from this situation as quickly as possible.

"Pleased to meet you, ma'am," he answered, stooping to pet Lucy before she hurt herself with her wriggling to remain still. "And call me Wiley."

This was what Mariah had been expecting: a midsixtyish man emanating the relaxed friendliness she'd encountered in her phone conversation with him. Wiley Albright was more spare in build than his nephew but had the same aqua blue gaze that sized her up just as Jeb's had seconds before. Then his eyes crinkled at the corners as he smiled at her and offered his hand with none of his nephew's reservation.

Slightly mollified, Mariah took it. For a minute there, she'd felt like a McCoy who had crossed onto Hatfield property. Or, she revised as she continued to feel Jeb's gaze on her, was she more like Blanche DuBois encountering Stanley Kowalski?

"Thanks for drivin' all the way here outside of regular business hours, ma'am," Wiley said.

"Accommodating myself to my clients' needs is my job. But really, I can't begin to imagine what two men living in God's country might need someone like me for."

"Yes, well..." Clearing his throat, Wiley tipped his head toward his nephew. "I guess you've met Jeb here?"

"In a roundabout way. At first I thought he was you, and he had no clue who I was." She turned toward the younger man, only to find him scrutinizing her with the same if not a greater caution than he had before.

"I hope you didn't have any trouble finding the place," Wiley said quickly.

She shook her head. "Your directions were perfect. That's probably why I was a little early. I like to leave myself a few extra minutes the first time I'm going to a client's house, in case I have to backtrack." Remembering Jeb's earlier doubt, she couldn't resist adding significantly, even if the point was probably moot, "It'd be rather difficult to show someone why they should depend on me to bring a harmony to their unsettled lives if mine wasn't in order."

"That's exactly what I thought when I saw you talkin' about what you do on the local cable hour last week," Wiley agreed with another glance at his nephew, whose countenance had grown, if possible, more guarded. And distinctly aggravated.

"Of course, organizing is just one of the things I can do," she went on almost challengingly, her gaze meeting Jeb's without falter, even if she wasn't sure why she would want to sell her services to a man who seemed to have little understanding or appreciation for what she was trying to do. "That's why I named my business what I did. I assist people in all kinds of ways tailored to their specific needs."

She didn't know why, but the next statement came out not with assertion, but revelation. "I like to think, too, that they need me to fill some function no one else can, because I truly care about making their lives more genteel...more civilized."

She was unaccountably wounded when Jeb, still piercing her with his gaze, showed no visible reaction to her heartfelt disclosure. Instead, he asked, "What's goin' on here, Wiley?"

"Time's running out, Jeb," the older man said rather defiantly. "I told you, you need to do somethin'. And soon."

"So you took it upon yourself to bring this woman out here to make sure I did."

Focused on her, Jeb's blue eyes grew brighter—and hotter—than the flame of a gas jet. Where on earth, she wondered, had she gotten her earlier impression he'd come to *any* appreciation of her? Because there was definitely none of that perception now, not even a close relation of such. Abruptly she was reminded of how she'd felt upon running into him: threatened on the most basic of levels. How she'd felt when encountering his probing, skeptical gaze, which heightened her sense of vulnerability—and not just physically.

The reminder provoked Mariah. On the most basic of levels.

"Either people perceive the value of my service, Mr. Albright, or they do not," she said coolly. "Clearly you don't."

And just as clearly, he wasn't fazed by her tone. No, Jeb Albright's eyes still held her, more thoroughly than his strong hands had earlier, a searching out of the truth that made her want to hide, or at the very least turn away. Which brought all of her feelings of peril flooding back.

"Just so we all know," he said, "what exactly is your business, Miss Duncan?"

"I'm…I'm…" Mariah could have cursed her hesitation, but for some reason unknown to her at that moment, she would have given anything not to have to tell him, "I'm from Saved by the Belle."

Chapter Two

Jeb didn't believe his ears, so he asked incredulously, "Saved by the *what?*"

Mariah Duncan lifted her proud chin in a way that both irritated and stirred him, which only increased his irritation. "Saved by the Belle. I'm a professional organizer with a Southern touch. My qualifications include a degree in liberal arts and six years' experience participating in nearly every aspect of some large philanthropic events in Dallas, as well as serving as a volunteer in several other capacities."

"Well, and dang if I wasn't just wondering where I'd find an ex-debutante to help me with my next charity ball," he drawled.

"It's not meant to be taken literally, Mr. Albright," Mariah retorted. "I assure you I am able to offer a wide variety of services I tailor to each client's specific situation. You might say I function like a combination of wife and secretary, doing the jobs they might. You know, the personal things everyone needs done for them now and then."

He couldn't help his reaction, he was just so aggravated.

And embarrassed to the roots of his being. Jeb raised one brow suggestively. "How personal?"

Mariah flushed. Oh, yes, he'd been right about those looks she'd been giving him, yet he wasn't all that gratified.

"Jeb," Wiley said warningly.

He shot his uncle a lethal look. Dad-blast Wiley! Here was the person who deserved being hit with both barrels. He could imagine the lead-in his uncle had given this woman: *Got a nephew here I can't see as ever sprucin' his ways up enough to be passable in polite society—or to attract a woman—and he needs to, real fast. So I figured it was time I took matters into my own hands and called in a professional.*

"Well, Miss Duncan," Jeb said, "sounds like you've got yourself a nice little concept there, but I don't think anyone here would begin to mistake needing the services of some charm-school-educated Southern belle."

She turned even redder, hugging her precious black leather date book tighter than a Bible. Then she lifted her chin a notch higher and said, with that starch in her voice he'd heard a couple of times already, "It's just a name. That's all."

It was his own statement thrown back at him, from when she'd asked him about Bubba J.'s. Well. Score one for the lady, he thought with grudging respect, even if her snooty tone nettled him. He could see why she resorted to loftiness, though. At about five-two and somewhere in the vicinity of a hundred pounds, Mariah Duncan probably had a hard time convincing anyone she had the muscle to solve their problems, since she looked as substantial as a bluebonnet in the breeze. And felt the same, he remembered, suddenly reliving the delicateness of her bone structure under his palms.

Yet her tailored slacks and silk blouse, casual while businesslike, did lend her an air of professionalism if not competence, as did the way she wore her cinnamon brown hair, pulled back in a sophisticated braid. The style also accented the purity of the fine features in her heart-shaped face, her skin pale and glowing as the pearls at her throat.

A face that reflected her apprehension of him, though she tried to hide it.

Remorse stabbed him. *Had* he hurt her with his rough handling, either physical or verbal? Certainly he knew he'd repulsed her with his fresh-from-under-a-rock aroma and that shower of lake water, courtesy of Lucy. Recalling her distaste made Jeb want to crawl under something for real. Of course, then there had been the patronizing way she'd asked him, all the while idly fingering the pearls Daddy had no doubt given her at her coming-out, if Jeb was Bubba J. As if she found the name—and him—a bit too hick to believe on first examination, but just so darn fascinating.

He'd heard that tone before, just as he'd seen that look.

Then he recalled, too, that Mariah had said she didn't know why Wiley had contacted her. Well, he'd be the last to fill her in on the matter.

"Begging your pardon, ma'am, for any disrespect or inconvenience in driving all this way for nothing, but my uncle clearly got the wrong impression of what your business does." He gave her a nod goodbye. "Have a nice evening."

"You're not even going to give the lady a chance?" Wiley spoke up.

"There's nothin' she can do for me," Jeb answered with a warning in his voice as he headed toward the store. He was not going to let his uncle take this conversation one step further.

Then from behind him, Wiley said, "What about Robbie, Jeb? You're gonna lose everything that matters to you if you don't do somethin'. You got a better idea of where to start?"

Jeb stopped. Turned. He loved his uncle like a father, but... "You're way outta line here, Wiley."

Mariah glanced from one to the other of them. "Perhaps it *would* be better if you both discussed the situation in private and then called me, if there's still a need for my services."

"Thank you for that consideration, Mariah," Wiley said, "but you're here now and I'd be next door to rude to send you off without an explanation. We owe you that, at least."

"Actually you don't—"

He put a hand on her forearm. "Stay, if you will, and listen to what my nephew's situation is. If there's even the slightest chance…"

"Well, all right," Mariah answered with obvious reluctance, and Jeb figured it was because of *his* rudeness she was feeling so, even though she regarded him with that expression he'd seen when she knelt at his feet petting Lucy. As if, despite being put off, she was willing to try to find a way to relate to him.

"Fine, then, Miss Duncan. Give us your expert opinion on the matter." Fixing his uncle with a look that could boil water, Jeb crossed his arms and said bluntly, "The situation is I've got exactly eight weeks before I stand up in front of a judge and try to convince him that an unmarried fishing guide and part-owner of an outdoors-supply business living with his bachelor uncle in a trailer out in the sticks can provide a proper, well-rounded environment to raise a kid in. I already know the obvious way to improve my case would be to take me a wife. The problem is, even if I was interested in gettin' married—which I'm *not*—I don't think it'd be a stretch to say livin' out here in this sort of setup isn't what a woman would find particularly appealing, for pretty much the same reasons."

He supposed exaggerating his good-ol'-boy accent wasn't going to win him any favors, but dad-*blast* Wiley for making him go through this! Jeb willed his face not to turn red at having to reveal details about his personal life to this woman, and went on, "So I assume what my uncle was thinkin' in his tangled-up way was that if I didn't have a wife or wasn't about to get one on my own, I could hire someone to help snare one by turnin' me into something that might appeal to a likely prospect, all in eight short weeks. And I'd be mighty surprised, ma'am, if miracles of that sort are part of the 'wide variety of services' you offer."

Comprehension dawned on Mariah's face. Out of the corner of his eye, Jeb saw that Wiley was thoroughly disgusted with him for deliberately painting the situation in such an unfavorable, and irretrievable, light. Well, he was just a tad disgusted himself—for caring what Mariah Duncan thought of him.

He waited for her to thank them both for the opportunity to do business but she couldn't help him. And off she'd go, back to her city living and her charities and clients and who the hell else that could use her brand of help.

Except it seemed she wasn't leaving. Not yet, at least.

"I don't quite see why you feel you need so urgently to change or take a wife," Mariah mused. "I mean, am I right in concluding that this Robbie you mentioned is your nephew?"

"No. That's the whole problem, y'see. Robbie is my—"

He was interrupted by a shout from up the hill. "Uncle Jeb!"

The three of them turned to see a girl, all jeans-covered legs and flying hair, running pell-mell toward them.

Robin—his niece.

Lucy galloped up to meet her, and girl and dog hailed each other like long-lost friends before racing the rest of the way home with the energy only the young have after a full day of activity.

Both came to a breathless halt in front of Jeb.

"I did it," bragged Robin, blue eyes shining as she looked up at him. "I mean, Wiley cashed out the register, but I swept the floor and put bait saver in the tank. I washed the fingerprints off the front-door window, and I even arranged the lures and cans of Skoal and Copenhagen in the display case."

"I'll bet they needed it." Jeb had to smile. Wiley, who minded the store most of the time, didn't think about such things. Not that their normal customer gave a hoot, but it was nice to have a touch of order, even if it was just neatening up cans of chaw.

He reached out and rumpled her hair. "Thanks, Robbie. Don't know what we'd do without you."

She grinned, a heartbreaking split in her angular face. She'd thinned out in the past few months—Jeb guessed because she'd sprouted at least an inch in that time, too. He'd have worried except she had the appetite of a pack mule. Hopefully she would fill out again, although it seemed impossible she'd ever grow into the coltish legs that were longer than the rest of her put together.

Yes, Robin was growing up fast, would turn eleven in just a few weeks. She'd become a real part of the family, and he had been tickled at the way she'd taken to the ins and outs of their distinctly male-oriented business. She had even begun imitating the pattern and inflection of his and Wiley's speech. And yet now, contrasting the two females, he saw how rag-tag Robin appeared against the polished and feminine Mariah Duncan. Almost as unkempt as he must look in comparison.

"I practiced my clinch knot, too," the girl chattered on. "I'm not near as good as you or Wiley at tying it, but maybe after school tomorrow I could try it on a real rig and see what I can catch. Wouldn't it be somethin' if I brought in another like that big ol' striper I caught this winter out near..."

Robin's smile faded as she finally noticed Mariah, who was studying the girl—and him.

Jeb put an arm around Robin's shoulders. "Miss Duncan, this is my niece, Robin. Robbie, uh, Miss Duncan.

She's here to...for...a visit." He gave both Wiley and Mariah a covert lowering of his brows that said *Let's not get into explanations.*

He should have known that Wiley would be oblivious to any message not spelled out on butcher paper in foot-high red letters. "Mariah's here to see about doing business with your uncle Jeb," the older man provided meaningfully.

This earned him an exasperated look from Jeb, even as Mariah smoothed the moment over with a warm "I'm pleased to meet you, Robin."

Jeb glanced down and noticed his niece's face had lost its earlier animation. She rested her weight on the outside edge of one cowboy boot, a thumb snared in her belt loop. Hooking an untidy lock of dark gold hair behind her ear, she solemnly regarded Mariah from under her lashes in a bout of shyness.

Then Jeb saw that Robin wasn't shy, but watchful. And he knew she'd come to the same conclusion about Mariah he had. It wasn't so farfetched. After all, the last time a woman dressed in professional clothes had shown up here, she'd been from the Department of Human Services and had given them the news that had triggered today's episode.

Damn. Jeb knew his niece had detected his worry these past few weeks, hard as he'd tried to hide it. Not that he hadn't kept her informed, in a simplified fashion. After all, she had a right to know about the situation, since it concerned her. But it was inevitable that she would look past his explanations and assurances and realize the real threat that hung like a thunderhead over them all.

A child shouldn't have to be afraid of such basic securities as home and family being taken away from her, Jeb thought, and he vowed not for the first time that somehow he'd think of a solution—a *practical* one, and not some harebrained idea that the answer to their woes could be found on the shopping channel!

At that thought, he lifted his gaze to find Mariah once again—or was it still?—studying his niece. And him.

"It sounds as if you're quite an angler, Robin," Mariah commented as though the girl had answered her greeting in kind, turning on that Southern charm that really was hard to dismiss as insincere. Hard to resist, too.

Robin's lashes flicked up for a quick look at Mariah, then down again. "I'm just learnin' still."

"Well, isn't that the way any one of us becomes an expert at what we do, by learning and practicing?"

This time Robin's gaze remained pinned on the ground as she confessed in a low voice, "Yeah, but...but I'm a girl."

Jeb's heart wrenched within him, a sensation of defeat before he'd barely started. Blast it, he was doing the best he could to make her feel she belonged!

Hoping the right words of reassurance would somehow magically spring to his lips, he opened his mouth. But Mariah again defused the awkward moment by asking, "Women can become practiced anglers, can't they? I mean, say I set my mind to it, I could succeed relatively well at it eventually, couldn't I?"

Robin blinked. "Well, sure, I guess..."

Jeb frowned, wondering the reason for such speculation by Mariah. He couldn't imagine she was serious about learning to fish, and he was positive his niece was having the same trouble as him in envisioning Mariah, with her refined demeanor and pearl necklace, hauling back on a fishing rig and whooping it up as she pulled a twenty-pound striped bass out of the water. Still, he saw the girl considering Mariah's remark.

Then Mariah added, "And just like any person finding themselves needing to learn how to do something outside their normal abilities, wouldn't it be shrewd to explore as many avenues of assistance as possible?"

Puzzlement suffused Robin's features, but even if she

didn't, Jeb definitely caught Mariah's drift—and her implicit criticism of him. Which made his irritation bristle up again. Where did she get off judging him? She didn't know a blamed thing about the situation!

Yet before he could voice his vexation, Robin said shyly, "I guess I might could show you a few things I learned from Uncle Jeb, if that's what you're gettin' at. But he's the expert on fishin'. And he can teach anybody. He's real patient and would never make you feel backward just 'cause a certain skill didn't come natural to you."

Jeb felt his chest swell at Robin's praise. Then when he saw Mariah smile approvingly and so very warmly at his niece, an even greater swell pulsed through him, nearly making him forget his annoyance with this woman.

Damn again.

And damn, too, if he'd let her make dewy-eyed fools out of any of them.

"It's true that when it comes to Texoma striper fishing, I'm your man." He met Mariah's gaze squarely. "But I doubt you really 'need' to learn to fish."

"Call it professional curiosity, then," she said. "Even if we eventually decide that I can't…do business with you, I'd like to hear the facts. As your uncle pointed out, the situation merits a deeper look, doesn't it?"

Jeb was on the verge of putting an end to the pretense that they were actually discussing fishing with a blunt disagreement when Mariah's eyes made him pause. He'd previously noted that they were golden brown and almond shaped, like a doe's. But what struck him now was the true interest in their depths.

Don't be a fool, he warned himself. There was no way this society silk stocking could even begin to comprehend their world—which hadn't even existed for her fifteen minutes ago—or a way of life so different from hers. How on earth could she help them?

"Go on inside, Rob. You too, Wiley." Jeb gave his

niece's shoulder a squeeze, a silent reassurance to counter
his sternness, which attempted to circumvent any protest
Wiley might be inclined to make. He furnished his uncle
with a glance, anyway, that brooked no argument. "I'll be
along as soon as I've seen Miss Duncan to her car."

Yet his uncle seemed content enough—or disgusted
enough—to depart without offering more of his opinions,
thank God. No, it was Robin who hesitated, her large blue
eyes darting from Mariah to him and back.

"I like your hair, Mariah," she blurted, as if she'd had
to force the statement out. Or perhaps couldn't prevent herself from expressing it. "Maybe…maybe if you do decide
to take fishin' lessons from Uncle Jeb, you could teach me
how to braid my hair like that."

"I'd like nothing more, Robin," Mariah answered
gently. "But that's up to your uncle."

His niece nodded, then did something he'd never seen
her do before: she gave her hair a girlish flip off her shoulder with the back of one hand before running off in her
tomboy clothes. And it became clear to him that she hadn't
been debating earlier what threat this woman might pose.
No, his niece had been wondering how she could get her
hair to look like Mariah's did!

Was Robin so starved for a feminine touch in her life
that a practical stranger could bring that longing surging to
the surface?

Wiley was right. Jeb needed to do something, more than
just take care of the situation looming on the horizon, in
order to do his best for his niece. And he knew it'd have
to be something definite—and drastic.

He wanted nothing to do with Mariah Duncan, though.
For all her highfalutin notions of believing she could, by
dint of her Southern gentility, make people's lives *civilized*,
he was certain there wasn't a single thing she could do for
him.

But if there was a chance for Robin's happiness…

Chapter Three

I must be out of my ever-loving mind, Jeb thought.

After Robin left, he stood for a few moments, fingers of one hand tucked in the back pocket of his jeans as he rubbed the palm of his other hand across his forehead, painfully aware that he was about to step way out of his comfort zone. Mariah was silent.

He squinted at the sky, the waning light making it a pale robin's-egg blue at its apex, the wispy clouds with their flamed undersides kicking up from the horizon like waves left in the wake of a boat.

"Let's take a walk," he announced, then in afterthought glanced down. "Or maybe not. Where I'm thinkin' of going is kind of uneven in places, and those shoes of yours don't exactly look to be made for a hike along the lake."

"Lead on," Mariah said gamely. "These flats will hold up."

"Fine." He wasn't about to talk her out of it. If she wanted the opportunity to put her two cents in, then she needed to know what she would be getting into.

With Lucy shadowing them, they tramped down to the

lake, then south along its rocky edge to a cove with a beach of sorts. There, Jeb dropped to a crouch and picked up a stone, rubbing its flat, smooth surface with his thumb. Perfect for skipping.

Lifting his arm to the side, he flicked his wrist, sending the rock flying. It leapfrogged across the water—one, two...five skips in all.

"I'm impressed," said Mariah, watching from her spot a few yards away.

He cut her a skeptical, sidelong glance, wondering if she was thinking such tactics would work on him—again. He couldn't tell; dusk was falling more quickly than he'd gauged, and Jeb became singularly aware he was alone with this woman in the burgeoning twilight.

"My personal best is nine skips," he said obligingly enough. "It's something I've always had a knack for. It used to irk Cody something terrible...." He peered into the darkness. The explanation wasn't going to be easy any way he did it.

"Who's Cody?" Mariah asked in that cultured drawl of hers he found almost mesmerizing.

Not looking at her, he answered, "My older brother—Robin's dad. He never was the outdoors buff I am. Or Wiley is. I didn't realize until years later that he must have felt like a fish out of water around us." Gesturing toward the lake, he gave an ironic snort at his comparison before sobering and going on.

"But Cody found his calling, eventually. Got a scholarship and went to A&M to become an engineer. So now the ugly truth comes out." Jeb paused dramatically. "Yes, I am the brother of an Aggie."

She gave a soft chuckle but wasn't going to let him off the hook. "What happened to him, Jeb?"

It was the first time she'd said his name, and it sent a shaft of that yearning he'd experienced previously shooting through his very vitals, making him believe more than ever that nothing good would come out of this interview.

He must remember, he was doing this for Robin. But he didn't have to tell Mariah everything, he reminded himself.

"Cody and his wife, Lisa, died in a car crash a little more'n four months ago," he said, forcing the words out. "I got custody of Robin. Right now I'm what the lawyers call Robin's temporary managing conservator." He pronounced it distinctly, carefully. "But I'm hoping to adopt her. That was to be decided once she'd lived with me six months."

He picked up another stone, tested its feel in his palm and discarded it. "Anyway, I knew if she got to live permanently with us two bachelors that there'd come a time when she'd need a feminine influence. A girl should have a mother, y'know."

"Of course, if it's at all possible. But do you think the court would take Robin away from you merely for lack of such influence on her?"

"Up to a few weeks ago, I didn't think so. Now there's more to the situation, you see," he went on with reluctance. "We were served with papers saying Lisa's half sister was coming forward to intervene for custody and adoption of Robin."

The thought of that action—and the implied impetus behind it—still had the power to upend Jeb's better judgment and raise panic in him, which he beat back with the aid of the indignation the situation unfailingly roused in him. With superhuman effort, he made himself go on, to tell Mariah the story.

But it would not be the whole story.

"Anita Babcock," he said flatly, "is Lisa's half sister. Her husband—he's an engineer, too, like Cody was, I guess—does some kind of work for an oil company that took them out of the country up until recently, but now they're back in the States to stay, or so I've been told. The judge kept the adoption hearing for June, even with the Babcocks intervening."

With sudden intensity, he jabbed a twig into the ground, almost to poke it into the heart of his dilemma. "From what the lawyer I hired tells me, as things stand right now, it could go either way. I could get Robbie—or Lisa's half sister could. I've definitely got the biggest advantage, with her livin' here with me and Wiley since Cody and Lisa died. But it's not like they named me Robin's guardian, which would have sealed the deal for sure. And Anita and her husband are already raisin' a couple of kids of their own, have the ability to give her all sorts of advantages— private school, lessons in just about anything Robbie might take a fancy to, travel, exposure to all sorts of experiences. Put that kind of home life up against the one I'm providing, and what would you decide if you were a judge?"

"I see..." Mariah frowned, her gaze distant, searching.

She still clutched her black leather organizer in her arms. He wondered if she ever went anywhere without it, and couldn't imagine being so tied to a schedule. Perhaps that was part of his problem, as she'd indirectly suggested, this reluctance to adapt to changing circumstances.

"And I gather from what you said earlier," she continued, "about your not being interested in getting married, that there's no one you're even seeing whom you might eventually consider...that is, for the judge to acquire some confidence you'd ultimately..." Her voice trailed off awkwardly.

"I take your meanin', and you're right," he said with a calm he didn't entirely feel. "I've known some women I've liked real well, and it's not entirely out of the realm of possibility that I'd find one some day that I'd want to settle down with, even given that my occupation doesn't afford much opportunity for socializing. After all, you can't tell what's bitin' till you test the waters. But things are different now—"

Jeb broke off. No, there was no reason Mariah Duncan needed to know this part of his predicament. No way was he going to discuss it with her, because it was the one aspect of this whole situation that had the least chance of being addressed.

Lucy, who'd left to forage in the brush on the water's edge, came trotting back over to see if he'd found anything more interesting, and Jeb occupied himself with locating a stick to throw, as if that were the reason he'd interrupted himself.

Again, though, Mariah wasn't buying his evasion. "How are things different now?" she asked with that sincere interest that pulled at him with tidal strength.

He chucked a short piece of driftwood into the water and watched as Lucy jumped in after it. He lifted one shoulder, feigning nonchalance. "I guess I feel it's my duty that whoever I eventually marry should be a woman like my sister-in-law was."

"And what was that?"

"Oh, you know—" he gestured vaguely "—a woman like yourself, brought up to be a lady, knowin' what's proper, who'd want to pass on such sensibilities to her daughter."

Jeb cleared his throat. He had never intended to stray into such deeply personal territory. And yet somehow he had.

"I don't mean to sound like Lisa couldn't let her hair down," he continued doggedly. "She was...genuinely nice. But it's not like that kind of woman would come lookin' for me."

Oh, but he was glad for the fading light now! He'd wanted to get that out, state the obvious to let Mariah know he knew the score. But when she didn't respond immediately and the silence stretched on, Jeb grew annoyed—with himself. Well, what did he expect? That she'd protest, say that of course women from all walks of life considered redneck fishing guides prime marriage material?

"Of course, even if a woman like that did come around, it wouldn't be right to marry someone just for the sake of marryin', regardless of my duty to Robin. And the truth is, I don't find that sort of woman, on the whole, real riveting, if you get my meaning," he put in pointedly—and not altogether truthfully.

Another lull pervaded the air between them as Mariah did not immediately respond. Jeb slapped at a mosquito, resolved he would reveal no more to her.

Finally, her voice distinctly strained, she said, "At least I can see now why you considered your uncle's calling Saved by the Belle to be an oversimplified answer to your predicament."

"Yeah, well. That's Wiley," Jeb said. So he'd made her uncomfortable with his indirect judgment of her. Welcome to the club, he thought, for he'd gotten an answer from her nonanswer. No, it didn't seem Mariah Duncan saw any way he might proceed from here. He couldn't help feeling aggravated, especially after she'd made such a big deal about hearing all the details. But she couldn't help him, not with this. He was on his own, just as he had thought.

Yet he couldn't prevent himself from feeling again the apprehensive tightening in his chest he'd experienced upon seeing his niece interact with Mariah. It was as if, even in that brief contact, there had passed between them something he could never fully understand. It struck him that Robin hadn't always been such a tomboy, had really only become so since moving to Texoma to live with him and Wiley.

Abruptly he stood, knee joints popping. "It's late. You'd better start back to town before you lose every scrap of daylight. I know you got here fine, but it won't be so easy in the dark."

Not waiting for her concurrence—or actually not wanting

to answer any more of her questions—Jeb left her to follow as best she could as he led the way back up the path and to her car. He did think to wait politely while she unlocked her door, and opened it for her with as much decorum as a man could muster while dressed in an overripe T-shirt and grungy jeans.

"Thank you again for driving out here," he told her formally.

"It was no trouble," Mariah answered, her voice subdued, as if she were a million miles away. She probably wished to be shed of him and this place, and again he wondered why she had even bothered to find out more about his situation with Robin.

He tried not to bear Mariah Duncan ill will. After all, it wasn't her fault that Wiley had called her here on a wild-goose chase. It wasn't her fault, either, that their problems couldn't be solved with one phone call.

"I hope you know my uncle's intentions were good. And I apologize for being unsociable toward you at first. I just didn't see, even then, that there was much you could do to help."

"I...I understand." Dropping her chin, she brushed the toe of her shoe through the twig-strewed dirt. "So what *will* you do about your situation?"

"That's the poser, isn't it? I'll keep on as I am already, I think, and just hope for the best. Let Robin know that Wiley and me...I...are her family and this is her home for as long as she needs it to be." He let his own gaze fall, thinking of his brother. "That we love her, which will never change. What else can I do?"

"What, indeed?" he heard Mariah murmur speculatively. Or was it skeptically?

"I mean," he continued, his tone defensive, "I know I could concentrate on givin' Robbie more occasion to act like a girl than a boy. I could stop calling her Robbie, for one," he admitted with a wry twist of his mouth. "And not encourage her so much to join in runnin' the business, even if she has taken to it like a fish to water...."

This time he didn't find his pun amusing.

As if reminded by his remark, Mariah said, "Oh, about Robin's request. What if I mailed her a book I have that shows how to do all sorts of braids and hairstyles with long hair?"

He was again surprised—and pleased. She hadn't forgotten his niece. "Robbie—Robin, I mean—would like that."

"You might help her at first, since it's easier if there's someone back there to hold the different sections of hair. That is, if you felt comfortable with that sort of thing."

Jeb shrugged. "How much more difficult could it be than snelling a hook?"

That brought out her smile, fleetingly, and the constricting band around his chest eased ever so slightly.

"I'm sure I wouldn't begin to know," she answered.

He knew Mariah hadn't been serious about him teaching her to fish, but Jeb suddenly wished for that opportunity to do so, because if there was one thing he did know backward, forward and sideways, it was fishing.

In that way, he and Mariah were alike, both involved in service businesses. But that was where the similarity ended. His responsibility was to produce tangible results; hers...not so apparent or defined. He felt he had the easier job of it.

"You know, I almost feel obligated to change the name of my business if I'm to adhere to truth in advertising," Mariah said.

It was as if she'd read his mind. "Well, it *is* just a name," he reminded her. "I bet you wouldn't find *everything* for fishing or camping at Bubba J.'s."

For some reason, she brightened at that, even gave a low, feminine, silvery laugh that oddly seemed to fit right in with the increasingly distinct night sounds around the lake.

But she wasn't here to fit in, which was as it ought to be.

"I'll wish you good luck, then, Saved by the Belle." He had yet to call her by her given name, and the omission served as a reminder as he found himself, against his very will, looking down at her and trying to memorize her features.

"Good luck to *you*, Jeb Albright," she said. And she held her hand out to him again.

Even though his own was no fresher than it had been when she'd extended hers before, something in his man's pride wouldn't let him balk this time. He took her hand in his.

It was soft against his palm, small and delicate. A woman's touch... The thought flitted through his head, bringing back that craving for...something—he didn't know what, only that it had gone unmet for years now.

His other hand covered hers, more complete contact with that softness—and in a test of sorts. He heard her short intake of breath as her other hand went to her throat again, fingers grazing across the pearls there as if touching a talisman. Yes, he saw the reaction he'd thought he would, that attraction that tugged at them both. Then her gaze flew up to meet his, doe eyes flaring slightly, as he felt in her grip the apprehension he'd first encountered upon seeing her. Or more accurately, her seeing him.

Immediately Jeb let go of Mariah's hand and stepped back. She said nothing but got into her car.

He stood there long after her red taillights had disappeared into the night.

So. She felt she wasn't being truthful in hiring herself out as Saved by the Belle. Well, he'd bet there were more than a few people out there looking for her kind of redemption.

He hated that the thought sent another torrent of longing ripping through him.

* * *

For the tenth time in an hour, Jeb flipped from his front to his back on the bed. It was going to be one of those nights, he guessed, of which he was having more and more lately.

This one was quite a bit different, though, for he wasn't just restless. He was edgy as a caged bobcat without its mate.

"Jeb?" Wiley whispered from the other side of the darkened bedroom. The mobile home had only two bedrooms, situated at opposite ends of the trailer. As a result, Wiley had given up his room to Robin and bunked on the extra twin bed in Jeb's room, vacated years ago by Cody. Jeb was only too happy to share, but sometimes Wiley snored like a hibernating grizzly. Or if awake, he talked, knowing he had a captive audience. Well, tonight Jeb was in no mood for confidences, not after today's fiasco.

"Jeb?" Wiley repeated. "You asleep?"

"Yep."

His uncle sighed. "You bein' surly with me ain't going to do anything more than earn you a second's worth of satisfaction."

Jeb hauled himself onto one elbow and peered across the room. "You don't think I have the right to be put out with you for pullin' that stunt today?"

"I didn't say that—"

"Well, then, what would you say?"

"I was just tryin' to help, son."

"Right. I know what you were thinking, Wiley, and it wasn't that Saved by the Belle could help any of us. At least not the way Mariah Duncan advertises she could. No, you saw her on that show and thought if you could just get her out here to meet me, lightning would strike us both, and there'd be the answer to all our troubles." That's what really chapped his hide about this whole deal. Wiley *knew* what had happened with Anita, and still he'd called Mariah out here.

The absurdity of it hit him afresh, as did every bit of his chagrin. "Good God, Wiley, what possessed you?"

"Well, there weren't no listing in the Yellow Pages for Saved by the Ign'rant Hick Uncle!" his uncle shot back. "Or believe you me, I'd've called the number on both our accounts!"

There was a moment of silence in the room before the two men burst out laughing. Jeb let his head fall forward, shaking it slowly. He never could stay mad at Wiley for long.

"Come on, now. Admit it. Didn't you think she might make as likely a candidate for a real fine wife and mother as anyone else?" his uncle asked.

"Miss Junior League? Yeah, right." All humor left him as Jeb scowled. "Besides, how could it possibly matter if I did?"

"I dunno. Seems to me I heard someone say a while back he'd try just about anything to keep Robbie." Wiley grunted as he rolled over, for the first time in Jeb's memory being the one to end the conversation, though not before delivering a parting morsel of food for thought, "You know, I always taught you and Cody that what you catch all depends on the bait you use."

And just who were you thinking was which in this case? Jeb thought but didn't ask. What would be the point? It didn't matter what his opinion was of Mariah Duncan, just as it didn't matter what she thought of him.

With a snort of self-disgust, Jeb flopped back on the bed, lacing his fingers behind his head and staring at the ceiling.

He had to admit, if only to himself, that the reason he'd been embarrassed at every turn today was because he *had* been attracted to Mariah Duncan, incredibly so, even with that touch-me-not haughtiness that put a man more in mind of a prim schoolteacher than a desirable woman.

Except he could tell, in that all-too-brief moment when

she'd been pressed against him, that she didn't lack for curves in all the right places. No, *ma'am*.

But it wasn't his fancy for her looks that had him tossing and turning. That he could acknowledge for what it was, as he recognized her own surface fascination with him. Oh, yeah, he'd seen that look before.

No, it was Mariah's demeanor that had socked him in the gut. How, he wondered, could he be even remotely captivated by some snobbish, butter-wouldn't-melt-in-her-mouth Southern belle? *Again?*

But there had also been Mariah's grace under fire, not to mention her continued kindness toward Robin even when he hadn't been much friendlier than a badger, twice as gamey smelling and three times as wild-looking. And given those factors, she still hadn't suggested it might be best for all concerned if Robin went to Lisa's half sister, Anita.

Yes…Anita Babcock. Now, there was a Southern belle. Aside from Cody and Lisa's funeral, he hadn't seen her in over fourteen years, and had never faced her here on his own turf until her visit a month ago. She and her family had been passing through DFW Airport on their return from whatever country they'd been residing in to their new home in Houston, had rented a car and "dropped in" to see Robin. It had been the first time, too, the Babcocks had seen where and how the girl was living. Which was fine with Jeb; he'd felt then and still felt he had nothing to hide or be ashamed of.

But Anita had picked the very day he, Wiley and Robin were spring-cleaning the store and boat house. The three of them had looked and probably smelled like something Lucy'd kept under the porch for a week.

And the result of that visit was that the Babcocks had come forward to say they simply couldn't ignore their duty to provide a more appropriate environment for Robin than her present one.

Dammit, why couldn't the woman leave him be? She'd

gotten what she'd always wanted out of life, hadn't she? A successful husband, two kids and a status life-style. Why must she now pass judgment on his?

But she had done so before, too.

Jeb stifled a sigh of frustration. Yes, he had only felt like this once before in his life—that who he was and what he did were not...enough. And the doubt had bombarded him repeatedly in the past two weeks since receiving the news about Anita intervening for custody of Robin.

With his edginess at a peak, Jeb flung back the covers and stood, clothed in his usual sleeping attire of a pair of briefs. He reached for the jeans he kept at the foot of his bed and slid them on before stepping out into the hallway and making his way to the kitchen. He was still unaccustomed to remembering to wear proper clothing in the common areas of the trailer, was used to walking about in or out of whatever he pleased as he had for the past twenty-five years. But that behavior wouldn't do with a young lady in the house.

Jeb was unusually conscientious about that aspect of his guardianship. He knew part of the reason the court hadn't waived the normal six-month period for awarding him adoption of his niece—as was often done in cases where the parties were related—was that of the very strikes against him thrown by Anita, now and fourteen years ago. He was a bachelor living with his own bachelor uncle in a trailer out on Lake Texoma, with no prospect of change.

Jeb filled a glass with tap water from the kitchen faucet, recalling how he'd stood here earlier this evening while doing dishes with Robin. They'd been almost through when she had spoken up, her cheeks flushing, about needing a permission slip signed for school. It was only after he'd read what she needed permission for that he understood her embarrassment at approaching him: the girls in her class were to see a film and presentation about puberty and how it would affect them.

At the bottom of the slip was the simple statement, "Mothers are invited to attend."

Jeb's fingers tightened reflexively around the glass. In the deepest corner of his heart, he had to wonder if a judge might not be right giving Robin to Anita. How quickly the girl responded to Mariah today told him a lot about Robin's need for a mother. Though she never said a word, he knew the girl missed her mother. What kid wouldn't?

He himself had been six years old when his parents had died, and he remembered Wiley saying once that when Jeb had come to live on Texoma, he'd been like a whelp weaned too soon from its mama. Cody had been older, and neither of their parents' deaths had impacted him the same way as they had Jeb.

So make that twice, he realized. Twice in his life he'd been made to feel that he had not been enough—enough to keep his parents from leaving him.

Maybe because Robin was older, she would adjust more easily, as Cody had. But he and Cody had been boys; Robin was a girl, and she was entering that age when a girl needed a mother most.

And not just *a* mother. A mother for Robin should be someone…naturally tender, with a combination of gentle strength and kindness. So kind and soft—

Abruptly Jeb tipped his head back and slugged down the whole glass of water in three swallows, as if to distract his mind from such thoughts. Crazy thoughts they were, showing him how desperate he was becoming. He'd told Mariah he wasn't going to take a wife just to give Robin a mother, but what if in doing so he managed to fill one or two needs of his own?

There were saner alternatives. Maybe his marital status wasn't going to change soon, but why couldn't he move the three of them—Robin, Wiley and himself—into town and take a job? He didn't know what on earth kind it would be, but at least Robin might take up more-appropriate interests than learning to bait hooks or gut fish. Wouldn't she be happier there, too?

Did it matter that something would die in him—and in Wiley—to leave here for the city?

Something would die in him, too, though, if he lost Robin.

Besides, Jeb had never dreamed of leaving the place he had come to as a grief-stricken orphan. He reckoned the reason he had set down such roots here, which continued to thrust ever deeper, was that as a boy, he had feared he would never have a place where he belonged again. That he would never be loved or needed. Memories of those fears were why Jeb encouraged Robbie to become involved in the fishing business, make her feel that it was part hers, too. To exclude her from joining in, from being a part of their family completely, would permanently disable a sense of hopefulness in the girl that had just barely learned to stand on two feet again.

Yes, he and Robin shared a special bond, having lost their parents and coming to live on Texoma with their only uncle. She was all either he or Wiley had left of Cody.

She was also all that Anita had left of Lisa. Sure, right now Robin was resistant to the prospect of living with her aunt, but perhaps that was because Robin didn't know Anita very well, she and her husband having been on the move so much. Maybe if Robin got a chance to get to know the whole family, see how she fit in, she'd feel differently. Maybe he would, too....

Dropping his chin, Jeb stared at his hand, barely visible in the dimness. Whether his fingers were turned white by the half-light or the way he gripped the edge of the sink, he didn't know.

But one thing he did know with soul-deep certainty: he simply could not lose that little girl.

Chapter Four

Nearly out of breath, Mariah entered the crowded bar where she was to meet Jeb Albright, painfully aware that she was late by a good twenty minutes. So much for impressing clients with your punctuality. Of course, Jeb wasn't a client; he'd merely called and said since he had to come into town this afternoon, perhaps they could arrange a place to meet and he could pick up the booklet she'd promised Robin. So this appointment was just a matter of convenience for them both, and Mariah had no reason to think it might be otherwise, although her brain raced with several possibilities. Almost as much as her heart.

For whatever reason, she hadn't been able to get Jeb Albright—or his niece, of course—out of her mind in the few days since she'd learned of their plight.

Then her pulse kicked up into another gear as she spied him. He was again dressed in jeans, these fairly new, though, and from the looks of them, as well fitting as the others he'd worn. His collared shirt, open at the throat, was clean and pressed but otherwise unremarkable. In this light, she saw that rather than dark brown, his hair was brunette shot through with gold highlights, and just as shaggy as it had appeared the other day.

As if he had heard her thoughts, Jeb looked up, catching her gaze, and ran a hand through those unruly waves. The action only marginally improved his hair's arrangement, making him seem a little less wild, although—strangely— no less appealing.

He'd been leaning back against the actual bar, fingers tucked into his front pockets, and he straightened at the sight of her, appearing both relieved and apprehensive at her arrival. As if one minute longer and he'd have bolted, appointment or no. She couldn't imagine why.

Unless there really was another reason behind this meeting.

"Sorry I'm late," she apologized once she'd made her way to his side. She caught the whiff of a spicy after-shave. Too much of it, she thought.

"No problem. I didn't have anything urgent to get back to."

Despite that assurance, he seemed a bit restless to be on his way. Vaguely disappointed, Mariah pulled the pamphlet out of her purse and handed it to him. "I've gone ahead and marked a few of the simpler braids to start out with."

"Good…good." Jeb nodded rather emphatically.

"And please, tell Robin she can keep it."

"Fine, I will. She'll like that." He stared at the booklet in his hands and shifted from one foot to the other. Definitely restless.

"Well, if that's all—"

"I…Would you like to sit down for a while?" he said on a rush. "I mean, have a drink? Although, we might have trouble finding a seat with the after-work bunch comin' in."

Mariah contained her surprise, along with the small jolt of pleasure his suggestion generated in her. "That would be nice."

Briefly he looked taken aback, as if he'd expected a different answer. Then he nodded again and, almost in afterthought, extended a hand in front of him. "After you."

Mariah took in the rustic surroundings and clientele as she scanned the admittedly overfull room for an open table. She'd never been to this establishment before, on the outskirts of Denison. It evidently catered to the blue-collar crowd—or actually, the T-shirted, Western-boot-shod and cowboy-hatted crowd, with a few billed gimme caps sprinkled throughout. Pitchers of draft beer seemed to be the beverage of choice. Smoke and the kick-it-out beat of a country song filled the air, making the place seem even more congested. Peanut shells crunched under the soles of her low-heeled pumps as she and Jeb made their way through the throng, most of whom stared frankly—and rudely—at her out-of-place attire, a pale peach linen pantsuit over a cream-colored shell of raw silk.

She jumped at the brush of his breath on her cheek as he bent to say into her ear, "I've only been here a few times, and I would've suggested a different place to meet you at, but I flat couldn't think of one. I don't come into town that often, y'see." He hesitated. "If you'd like, we can go some place else that's more, you know, your style."

"No, every place in town is just as packed this time of day," Mariah told him, pulling away from him. But the crowd's scrutiny made her a little jittery. Or maybe it was the scrutiny of a man who'd claimed he didn't find women like her "real riveting." Of course, he'd been speaking of his late sister-in-law, but Mariah had caught his meaning. And despite herself, such judgment of her had hurt, even coming from the kind of man she might least expect to understand.

"This is fine," she said tightly, her pleasure at his unexpected invitation waning. "Really."

Turquoise blue eyes marked her expression, and he answered with his own tight "Whatever you say."

Finally they spotted a table, a tiny one back in the far corner. Taking the chair next to the wall, she pushed back her hair. She'd only recently taken to wearing it down on occasion, or in one of the less traditional braids. Then she recalled Jeb's other remark about his late sister-in-law, of her being able to let her hair down once in a while. She hastened to explain, ''I was at a soccer match.''

''A soccer match?'' With difficulty, Jeb squeezed into the chair next to her. Elbows bumped, knees brushed, gazes collided in unspoken apology and she became physically even more aware of this man.

So nothing had changed for either of them. Jeb Albright still had every bit of that tangible sexuality she'd perceived the other day. But what struck Mariah now was how that image continued to lure her in. Abruptly the feel of his roughened hands holding hers was revived. There had been an earthy honesty in that touch, uncultivated but quite genuine, and she experienced again the apprehension it had raised in her—that such sexuality had a power that could not be denied.

''The son of one of my clients plays in a junior soccer league,'' she found herself babbling, in an attempt to escape her thoughts, ''and I videotape his games. Both parents work in Dallas and find it difficult to get away for the matches.''

Scooping her hair over one shoulder to finger-comb it into order, she continued with some pride, ''Watching a tape isn't as good as being there, but they tell me it's become a family ritual, with full commentary and instant replays. Apparently the boy thinks he's living the best of both worlds, getting to sit at his parents' sides as they watch him play.''

''You can actually make a livin' doing that? Taping the kid's games, I mean?'' Jeb asked, his expression one of amazement—or skepticism, which called up their inauspicious first meeting, when he'd been so dubious of her ability to help him.

"I run a service business. Which means, as I said before, I do whatever seems to fit the client's particular needs," Mariah answered ever so politely.

Apparently oblivious to her defensive tone, Jeb continued to scrutinize her with that same speculative expression, which succeeded in provoking her even more.

"Can I get y'all something to drink?" A waitress in a tube top and hot pants stopped next to their table.

"Yes, I—" Mariah glanced up and suddenly found herself reliving a past moment. One with her ex-husband, Stephen—or actually it was him with just this sort of woman, a big-haired and busty truck-stop waitress, entwined on the living-room divan.

Why was she having this flashback now, when she hadn't for months? Mariah wondered. Of course, until now she'd had no reason to make comparisons. No cause to be made to feel lacking, and wouldn't feel so now if it weren't for Jeb Albright.

Raising her chin, Mariah answered coolly, "A mineral water, if it wouldn't be too much trouble."

"No more than usual." The woman scratched the order on the top cocktail napkin stacked on her tray before giving Jeb the once-over. Leaning one palm on the table, she treated him to a friendly, gum-cracking smile. "And for you, darlin'?"

Jeb's lashes flickered in subtle examination of the waitress's cleavage—or at least that's how it seemed to Mariah. Of course, he could hardly avoid it. "The same," he ordered.

"Oh, please," Mariah told him. "Don't let my not having a drink keep you from having one."

His eyes cut to her, then to the waitress. "No, thanks."

"Really, you mustn't put yourself out on my account. Isn't that why you wanted to come to this particular establishment, for the pitcher specials?" She clasped her hands in her lap and gave him a tight smile. "What man doesn't look forward to having a cold one or two after a full day of fishing?"

"With my old man," the waitress quipped good-naturedly, "he's more like to be lucky if he's got a fish or two after a full day of drinkin'."

She chortled at her own riposte, but Mariah saw at once that Jeb was not amused. Voice devoid of all of its Texas twang, his pronunciation precise, he told the waitress, "Two mineral waters, please."

The woman gave a miffed shrug. "All right, don't get yer shorts in a twist. Two mineral waters comin' up."

She elbowed her way elsewhere, leaving them in the midst of another uncomfortable silence. Mariah garnered no satisfaction from her little put-down as the awkward moment only drew itself out, with Jeb covertly glancing toward the exit. In fact, she felt ashamed of herself, regretting the brief annoyance that had made her act so insensitively. So…sanctimonious, as if she were unable to fathom how one could fall prey to such base weaknesses of the flesh. It *wasn't* her—no matter what Stephen might have contended. There was definitely something about Jeb Albright, though, that brought out the defensiveness in her, as she'd seen herself do the same in him.

She didn't understand. And it suddenly became very important that she try to.

"Tell me—what's so wrong in suggesting you have a beer?" she asked.

In a flash, Jeb had turned toward her, sliding one forearm along the back of her chair, setting the other on the minuscule table so that she was effectively boxed in. She wouldn't have needed to see those blue eyes shooting sparks to know he was furious. It radiated from him.

"I don't drink," he said evenly, "not even on my own time. For one, fishing is my business, and my business depends on my reputation. I can't afford even the slightest whiff of a doubt that I can be trusted with people's lives, and there's always that danger. Second, despite popular belief that fishin' is just an excuse for a bunch of party-hearty rednecks to guzzle beer all day, it *is* serious business, and I do not allow alcohol of any sort on my boat. Sure, everybody's just enjoying a pleasant day out on the lake, but I've seen too many accidents caused by carelessness or ignorance alone. When you put alcohol into the equation, I can just about guaran-damn-tee that sooner or later somebody's gonna get hurt.''

Even though she still didn't entirely understand what fueled it, Mariah didn't flinch from the righteousness in his words or the unvarnished anger in his gaze, which imprisoned hers as surely as his position practically pinned her against the wall. Yet both emotions were too honest not to confront head-on, compelling her to be as frank in return.

"It was never my intent to depreciate what you do for a living, Jeb," she said softly but with total conviction. "Any more than you might have intended to do the same by asking me how I could make mine rendering the sort of services I do."

Mariah actually saw comprehension of her words fill those aqua eyes, tempering their laser intensity, changing the emotion expressed there. And what it changed to was respect—albeit as grudging as the crooked smiles this man tended toward, it was still definitely respect.

Now oblivious to the pounding cacophony of noise surrounding them, Mariah found an emotion or two of her own blooming in her. It was the way he looked at her, as she'd thought he had before, with an appreciation for what she was trying to do in her business, maybe even for who she was. It was what she had been striving for since her divorce, in both her personal and professional life. Wasn't it?

"I apologize for again takin' my frustration out on you,"

Jeb finally said in a low voice. "I surely didn't ask you here to do so. It's just that..."

Yes, some urgent purpose had driven him to seek her out, for Mariah was now certain there was more motivation behind this meeting than him obtaining the promised pamphlet for his niece. Her curiosity escalated, as did the not altogether sane hope that he *might* need her—her services, that was. It certainly seemed his opinion of her had changed since the last time they talked, just as seeing him interact with his niece had changed her perception of him, too, from contentious Johnny Reb to...to what?

"It's just that we're very different people, aren't we?" she finished his sentence, trying to bridge the gap between them. Needing to, for her own understanding. "Different upbringing, different experiences in life and..."

"And?" Blue eyes bored into hers, searching. She was suddenly put in mind of the saying about the eyes being the windows to a person's soul. Except with Jeb Albright it was as if the curtains had been thrown back and the blinds raised, making what he saw through those eyes as clear as what was seen.

And exactly what did he see when he looked at her?

"But that doesn't mean we can't...respect each other's position, does it?" Mariah said, faltering. "Even if we don't completely understand—or agree?"

At her question, he searched her gaze a moment longer. Then he sat back in his chair, as if discouraged. He nodded once, slowly, then more firmly. "You're right. And if someone finds himself needing to step into a different world to learn something, it doesn't necessarily mean he's got to embrace every bit of that world, does it?"

Mariah waited for him to elaborate. Even after their drinks were delivered, some time passed before he spoke, his concentration centered on turning his glass around and around on the tabletop. "I guess I'm finding it hard to accept that Wiley was right, and I should get some help with Robin.''

"I don't know about that. She's a sweet girl, you know."

"Yeah, but is that gonna be enough?" He lifted his glass but didn't drink, only stared at its contents, frowning. "Actually I'd thought it was—until I saw Robin's reaction to you, saw her and you in contrast.... You know, she hit the nail right on the head when she wondered if she'd ever be much of an angler—not 'cause she's a girl, but more whether she should be devotin' that much time to such an activity. And you hit the nail on the head, too, when you asked how anyone gets to be an expert at somethin' except by learning and practicing. Part of me says to leave well enough alone, that I can't change the way I...can't change things enough to make a difference in two months. But part of me knows that if I did nothing and I lost Robbie—''

His fingers clenched around the glass, just as Mariah felt her heart contract in sympathy for him. Yes, this man and his niece had made quite an impression on her the other day.

"It isn't a certainty, by any means, that the court will give Robin to the Babcocks. After all, the girl's been living with me for four months. This environment is what she's used to, and the lawyer says most judges are reluctant to subject a kid to more change than absolutely necessary. But he also said that in determining a permanent home for Robin, some judges place more weight on the sort of situation the child's come from. In that case, the Babcocks are the likely pick. It all has to do with the 'best interests of the child,' the lawyer said. And only the judge can decide how those interests'll be best served.''

His brow furrowed as he talked. "The court's appointed a *guardian ad litem*—a social worker who'll be doing a home study of both living situations about two weeks before the hearing. I guess the judge places a lot of value on the social worker's report, and this woman'll be taking a good look at the environment Robin's living in and all. There'll be interviews with Robin and me and probably Wiley, or so's my understanding. Like I told you the other day, it's pretty certain I'm not going to be furnishin' Robin with a mother before then who might provide a feminine influence on my niece—and who might give a judge some confidence that the girl would be raised in a more well-rounded environment. But now I'm thinkin' if I showed the social worker how I was willin' to do whatever it took to fill any gaps in Robin's upbringing, maybe she'd be inclined to look favorably on that effort and recommend custody of Robin be given to me."

At last his eyes lifted and met hers, and the need in his gaze took her aback, for it *was* quite tangible. "And for that I've got to have you, Mariah."

She swallowed. "You do?"

"Yes. To help me with Robin. Now, I don't expect you to work miracles in barely two months." He took a deep breath. "What I was thinking was that you could give me some guidance on showing Robin how to act more like...like a lady, is the only way I can think to put it, even if the word brings to mind kind of a high-and-mighty image."

"I see," she murmured, then asked carefully, "As I am 'high-and-mighty'?"

"I don't know that I'm a fitting judge of such things." Jeb took a quick gulp of mineral water as if to douse the flush of fire that crept across his cheekbones before going on determinedly, "I'm just tryin' to face the facts. And one of 'em is, I am what I am—a man raised by my uncle without a lick of feminine influence. And without much for niceties. Which was fine for my brother and me—" his lashes dropped briefly, as if he stifled an internal pain "—but not for Robin. That's why I'm comin' to you."

Now it was Mariah's turn to fool with her drink, jam the swizzle stick into a depression in one of the ice cubes, focus on any bit of business rather than meet Jeb's too-discerning gaze.

He wanted to teach his niece how to be a proper lady. Strange that he should use that word in particular. Suddenly they weren't Jeb's words but Stephen's that echoed in her brain: *You're a real lady, Mariah. A true Southern belle, the kind of woman I want at my side. It's why I married you. But sometimes a man has certain…needs. Needs a woman raised like you were can't understand—or fulfill.*

Perversely, Mariah had agreed with Stephen. She *hadn't* understood, would never understand how a man could rationalize away his cheating as being a perfectly natural human condition. Oh, she believed him when he'd said he would give up his truck-stop tart if Mariah had wanted him to, as if that would resolve the matter. But she'd believed, too, that while he might end it with that particular woman, there would be another somewhere else down the line, for as long as Stephen continued to feel some need of his was going unmet in their marriage, he'd keep roaming.

Though feeling hurt and betrayed, she'd been willing to try to save the marriage. Yet when she'd tried to get him to explore what problem in their relationship led him to seek physical satisfaction outside of it, to explore what they both might do to fulfill each other more, he'd changed from patronizing to shocked to censuring. Hadn't she heard a word he said? She was his wife, a *lady*—not some cheap, rabbity trash! He didn't know why she was making a federal case out of him having a girl on the side, anyway. Wasn't he providing her with everything *she* could possibly want: the opportunity to do her charity work, her place among her society friends, money to buy whatever she desired?

But she hadn't wanted Stephen's money or social status. She'd wanted his love and respect, wanted him to love *her* for who she was, not because she was—or *wasn't*—a certain "kind of woman." And wanted him not so much to appreciate who she was as…desire her for being so.

Mariah ducked her head, as if Jeb's too-direct gaze could have detected such thoughts. She knew in her heart she'd acted as she must, with as much dignity and grace as humanly possible, asking for nothing from Stephen when she divorced him. She wasn't left destitute, by any means; she had money of her own with which to make her way, as she was determined to do. She'd left Dallas and the society "friends" who now considered her, a single woman, a threat to their own marriages, and moved to the Sherman-Denison area, which promised an excellent market for her new service business. Her only slip to Stephen's level had been in defiantly naming her business Saved by the Belle— an indiscretion she had regretted on more than one occasion, most notably right now with Jeb Albright.

In her mind, though, Mariah was nothing so antiquated as a Southern belle. But Saved by the Belle wasn't just a name, either, as she'd told Jeb; it was a not very subtle and not entirely estimable dig at Stephen. Regardless, she'd chosen this particular career path to prove to herself more than to Stephen what she so strongly believed: that there *were* people in this day and age who appreciated the ideal of Southern standards and values with which she'd been raised.

And Jeb had obviously taken that aim to heart—in the context of his niece. Even if she perceived a certain improbability for success in his plan, it made some sense for him to come to her to execute it. And yes, she had a reasonable assurance she would be able, at the very least, to help him smooth out some of the rough edges in his approach with the girl.

But what if she was unable to really help them constructively? There was so much at stake here. A little girl's happiness. What really could she impart to Robin, who'd already endured the cruelest of disappointments, that would help her?

"I don't know, Jeb," Mariah finally said, still not looking at him. "I'd have no way of measuring how successful my efforts are, except in whether you're permitted to adopt Robin. And if you're not, well…"

She ventured a glimpse at him. He was staring at her, jaw set obstinately. "You don't think I can do it, do you? You don't think I have it in me to learn how to raise a young lady. And I shouldn't even try."

"That's not it—"

"If it is me that's the problem, I give you my word I'll cooperate to the best of my abilities."

He gave her one of his wry half smiles, and she began to grasp the real reason for her reluctance to accept this assignment.

"I may be kinda rough around the edges, but I do have *some* sense of propriety and I promise to use it."

He set one clenched fist on the table, resting it upon the booklet he'd be taking home tonight to his niece. "All I know is that more and more I'm feelin' at a loss in seeing to Robin's needs, not just in giving her the amenities of a gentler upbringing, but as a…a growing girl. And I can't fail her there."

She stared at him helplessly. Such resolve he had, to do, as he'd said, whatever it took to see to his niece's best interests. How could she fly in the face of such purpose when truly he was asking her to carry through on her own commitment in starting up Saved by the Belle?

Would she be doing so, though, Mariah wondered, to validate something in her own mind rather than to help Jeb and Robin? Would it be wrong if she was able to do both at the same time?

Some of her dilemma must have shown on her face, for Jeb leaned forward urgently, his hand sliding across the table toward hers. He stopped, though, just short of touching her.

"Work with me," he pleaded softly, simply. "Please, Mariah."

Oh, yes, there was a definite allure in such plain honesty, and Mariah would have had to have been made of stone not to be influenced by it. For finally it was no purpose, noble or self-serving, that turned the tide. No, it was the way he said her name, deep and drawling and ever so sincere—*M'riah*—that made her see she simply couldn't turn away again from this man. In a way it terrified her, that she could be so helpless to do his bidding. But it also recalled her to the true purpose of her business—to help people make their lives easier, better, more civilized.

She *did* believe in that purpose, however she might go about upholding it.

Still, Mariah wondered what she was letting herself in for emotionally, even as she agreed, "All right, Jeb. I'll help you and Robin. Or try my best, at the very least. I must tell you I don't have a clue about where to go from here, but I guess I'll think of something." She gave a rueful laugh. "After all, I do bill myself as gearing my services to my client's personal needs."

Too late she recalled similar words, when she'd promised to provide a personal touch in her business—and Jeb's provocative *How personal?*

Yet there was nothing suggestive in his expression as he pressed his lips together and gave a firm nod. As if now he knew with certainty there weren't the least grounds for such a suggestive response.

He couldn't believe he'd taken Miss Scarlett O'Hara to a kicker bar.

Jeb downshifted ruthlessly, causing his pickup's gears to screech in protest. He eased up on the accelerator in apology. But *damn* it was hard not to take his disgust with himself out on something.

He had realized shortly into his conversation with Mariah this evening that he'd been holding out a secret hope he might not have to bring up his proposal to hire her. Crazily he'd fostered the most remote of fantasies: that in this meeting, with just the two of them and without the setting and situation of Texoma to stress their contrasts, he and Mariah might discover they had a lot in common.

But in his fantasy, he would have taken control. He'd have asked if she'd like to explore the subject over dinner, and the evening would have continued as smoothly. And when it was over, he might have even walked her to her car, leaned her up against it and kissed those lush, full lips of hers with such knowingness she'd have wondered aloud how any difference between them could matter when there was this.

And in that moment, he'd have believed he had a chance, with her at his side, of keeping Robin. Of being...happy.

Despite himself, Jeb gave the gearshift a convulsive yank into third, because the fact was, he'd sat there like a knot on a log barely able to put two words together—that was, aside from when he'd let loose with his little lecture on how noble was his calling to be a fishing guide. It hadn't taken long after that for it to become abundantly clear he'd been correct in his initial judgment: she found him less than impressive, even while still harboring her sheltered-miss fascination with this country boy. And in the end, he'd used that attraction to get what he wanted, a ploy of which he wasn't entirely proud.

Yet he couldn't be quite contrite for taking such advantage. He'd have done much more to improve his chances to keep Robin. Not that this plan would absolutely ensure such an end, for even with coaching, he had no delusions he'd ever be able to meet Robin's particular feminine needs. Yet at the thought of her ending up like that brassy, brazen waitress—or worse, in his mind, like haughty Anita Babcock—he'd try anything.

He had to believe Mariah would be able to strike that balance. He didn't see how he had much choice but to hire Saved by the Belle. Didn't have much choice, if he wanted to keep Robin, than to seek Mariah's special kind of care—

Once again Jeb took a cut from that acute longing he'd experienced the other day, for suddenly he saw not the road ahead of him but Mariah as she'd looked today, her cinnamon brown hair loose and waving around her face, big, doelike eyes looking like two tarnished pennies in the dim, smoky light as she gazed at him. She'd looked strangely untouchable and approachable at the same time. Wise in the ways of the world, while still innocent. Cautious, while still herself needing to reach out and believe in something.

Most likely the reason he kept seeing such opposites in her was because of that crazy name she'd given her business. Saved by the Belle, which called up an image of a hothouse flower refusing to wilt even under the force of the harsh Southern sun. Maybe that was where they'd come up with the expression *steel magnolia,* meaning the kind of woman who exuded quiet strength and kindness. A woman to whom people turned for guidance and support, as he just had, even as she needed protection. All the love and protection a man could give...

He was the one who was crazy to put himself in the position of seeing Mariah again. But if she helped Robin, it'd be worth it. And he was doing this for Robin.

"Yeah, who'm I foolin'?" Jeb snorted.

The gears gave a groan of protest. This time he laid off of them, since he'd reached the straightaway leading down to Bubba J.'s. That didn't stop Jeb from roundly cursing the truck's transmission for being so touchy. Or Wiley for butting in and getting them mixed up in this mess in the first place.

Or himself most of all.

Chapter Five

Disbelieving bafflement. Mariah could see it in Jeb's eyes, making him look like a man in front of a firing squad with no notion of what he'd done to put him there. Sort of a *How did I get into this and how on earth am I going to get out of it?* look. Of course, she didn't know a man who wouldn't rather be shot than face a roomful of giggling, squealing eleven-year-old girls.

But face them he did as Robin dragged him by the arm into the mobile home's small living room, where her birthday slumber party was being held—and where total chaos seemed to be reigning. Having arrived in the past half hour, most of the girls had done nothing more than toss down their sleeping bags and overnight totes and greet each other excitedly.

Now, however, the furor died down, Mariah noticed, watching through the conversation window between the kitchen and living room. With shy excitement and a certain pride, Robin was introducing her uncle to the assembled group of five.

"And this is Katy Dukes, and this is Daisy Underwood,"

she finished, hooking a lock of her dark blond hair behind her ear. One of the first things Mariah had done in her role of smoothing out the girl's rough edges was to have Robin's hair reshaped, so that now she had a few bangs to soften the angularity of her features and bring out her large blue eyes. Much anticipated for later on was a hair-braiding demonstration, courtesy of Mariah.

Playing host and both parental roles for the evening, though, was Jeb, and he assumed his function admirably, saying, "You must be Art Underwood's girl. I've taken your dad and a few out-of-towners from his bank out for some fishing on occasion. He caught a beaut of a seventeen-pounder last time, if I recall correctly."

Rolling her eyes theatrically, young Daisy groaned. "He *still* talks about it! One time he went on about it, like, *all night.*" Then she giggled, blushing, as if amazed at her cheekiness. Clearly even adolescent girls were not immune to Jeb Albright's intense, blue-eyed gaze.

But he didn't notice, had already turned that gaze to Robin, and she to him, as they did what Mariah had come to think of in the past few weeks as their approval check. She had first encountered the situation when she and Jeb had taken Robin shopping a few weeks ago for more-appropriate clothes than the T-shirts, jeans and cowboy boots the girl favored. After some hesitation, Robin had gotten into the spirit of things, picking out some lovely outfits, including the mint green tunic top with green-and-white checked leggings she wore right now. Then she had looked to Jeb for confirmation that whatever had been decided or was happening met with his favor. And he returned the look, both seeming half-puzzled, as if uncertain what was expected of them but wanting so very much to do right by the other.

Such devotion between this man and his niece brought a lump to Mariah's throat, and she turned back to her task of emptying corn chips into a bowl to hide her reaction. She wondered how, really, she'd be able to help these two.

It definitely wouldn't be for lack of trying on Jeb and Robin's parts. They'd been real troupers so far in executing her makeshift plan, such as it was. Mariah and Jeb had decided she would come out to Texoma twice a week, arriving around the time Robin got out of school and staying until five or so in the evening. It was as much of her time as Jeb felt he could afford and, besides, he was in the middle of his busiest season, with a schedule that was demanding, to say the least. Mariah had discovered he worked seven days a week this time of year, rising at two each morning and retiring by seven at the latest in the evening.

She could see, as he'd claimed, how he wasn't left with much time for socializing. Or for dating.

"So how many more hours of this am I in for?" Jeb murmured into her ear, making Mariah jump. She turned her head to find him close behind her, his broad shoulders almost filling the tiny kitchen as he reached around her for a chip. Munching it meditatively, he leaned a hip against the edge of the kitchen cabinet while she tried not to slop salsa all over the counter as she poured it from its jar to a bowl. Somehow he had a way of making her feel all thumbs. As if her edges were the ones needing a good smoothing out.

Tonight he smelled neither of silty lake nor too-strong after-shave, but of clean, warm-blooded man. His hair was still damp from a shower and brushed straight back, the bangs curving around his temples, ends catching in his thick eyebrows and eyelashes.

"Well, it's what, six-thirty now?" she prattled. "You serve tacos at seven, presents are opened shortly thereafter. Cake and ice cream at eight or so. Pop the movie you rented into the VCR while they're eating. That means it'll be fairly quiet for a couple of hours. I suspect then it'll be time for a game or two. After that, if I remember my adolescence correctly, a séance and/or boy talk."

Jeb's gulp was audible. "And I'm expected to be involved in all this?"

Mariah tried to hide her smile, unsuccessfully. "Heavens, no. You're expected to keep the food and soft drinks coming and stay out of sight, except maybe to come out of your bedroom once or twice during the evening and warn them to pipe down. I doubt that particular duty is one you'll need crib notes for, though. The noise will be deafening."

He cocked one skeptical eyebrow. "Will be?" he asked over the din emanating from the living room. Still, he seemed not particularly perturbed. "You've done a great job preparing and planning Robin's party. I'm kinda surprised, really." He indicated the chips and salsa. "I guess I was expecting a tea party with white gloves or something. But this seems just about perfect for Robin, Mariah."

As was the case for the past three weeks, it seemed she subconsciously held her breath until the next time he said her name in that sensual way of his—*M'riah*—and she let the air out of her lungs in a sigh. Now the process could start all over again. "That's where the personal touch comes in." She couldn't prevent herself from giving him that gentle reminder.

"So it does," he acknowledged without rancor. "Well, it sounds like you've got my work cut out for me, if you need to be going."

"I've promised to do the girls' hair." She rearranged a stack of napkins unnecessarily. "I don't mind staying, anyway, no charge."

"Well, that'd be fine." She thought she heard pleasure in his voice. "That reminds me—when does the slumbering part of this gig come in?"

"You didn't know?" Mariah gave him a long look.

"Know what?"

"The object is not to slumber but to see who can stay up the longest."

"You mean they're going to go on, like, *all night?*" Jeb asked drolly and rolled his eyes in a perfect imitation of Daisy Underwood.

She couldn't help it; unexpectedly charmed, Mariah giggled—exactly as Daisy had. Jeb gave a soft laugh in return, white teeth gleaming in his tanned face as he smiled one of his lopsided, single-dimpled smiles. You could have put a dime in that dimple and it'd have stuck.

He looked somewhat surprised but pleased that he had been able to amuse her so. Admittedly Mariah was used to Stephen's brand of wit, which tended more to sarcastic understatement than mimicry. How, she wondered not for the first time, had he found that waitress at all interesting?

But of course, scintillating conversation hadn't exactly been what Stephen was after. More like cheap thrills.

As she was thrilled by Jeb's riveting blue eyes?

Nonplussed, Mariah grabbed the bowls of chips and salsa and turned, ostensibly to set the food on the barlike ledge between kitchen and living room, but actually to try to control some of the heat that had risen in her like a wildfire at such thoughts.

Glancing up, she caught Robin's measuring gaze, so like her uncle's, upon her, reminding her she was not here to be either charmed or thrilled.

"How about I do that braiding demonstration now while you girls are having a snack?" Mariah asked distractedly, and braced herself as the youngsters shrilled their agreement and pounced on the chips.

Later, remaining in the background as the activities flowed into each other, Mariah continued to dwell on the matter of what Robin might think of her—or her function here. She and Jeb had told the girl a version of the truth: that Mariah was here to provide Jeb with guidance on how to be a proper parent to a girl, thus prompting Robin's cooperation. So far they'd gotten her enrolled in music lessons, had even rented an upright piano, which seemed to take up an inordinate amount of space in the already cramped living room. She'd pursued the matter of personal grooming even further, and had begun reacquainting Robin with some of the finer points of style and manners. And since up to five months ago, the girl had been reared in a more traditional atmosphere, the change was rather swift and dramatic, making Mariah's job less difficult on that score.

As for sprucing up the setting, Mariah had also encouraged and guided Robin in redecorating her bedroom, and the girl had shown her enthusiasm by picking a scheme incorporating her school colors, which thankfully were royal blue and white. Yet whenever a suggestion for modification was brought up by Mariah, the girl looked to her uncle first, silently asking whether this was what *he* desired or thought best, reinforcing Mariah's suspicion that Robin's enthusiasm stemmed more from her desire to please her uncle than any real love of pretty things.

But it was one step closer to making Robin more genteel, as Jeb had deemed his niece should be. And for Mariah, one step closer to proving that there was a place in today's world for such values.

"Tired?" Jeb asked, startling Mariah from her musing. "Why don't you go on home? I can probably handle it from here on out."

She glanced into the living room where the girls were eating their dessert and watching *Little Women* on video, having given their gifts to Robin. She had received some beautiful presents, including a sheet-and-comforter set for her bedroom that Mariah had picked out as Jeb's gift to his niece. Mariah had watched the girl's changeable features go from delighted to contemplative to ambivalent.

Confusedly Mariah couldn't help feeling she was failing even as she succeeded.

"I...I guess I am a little tired," she admitted. She glanced up at him. "You looked bushed yourself, and you've got a pretty early morning of it tomorrow."

Wiley had retired already, having volunteered to do Jeb's normal job of catching bait, which would allow Jeb to sleep in until five or so, when the customers would arrive for their morning of fishing. The plan then was for Wiley to feed the girls a breakfast of his homemade waffles and afterward keep them from getting into trouble until various parents came to pick them up around midmorning.

"I can handle it," Jeb said with a shrug. "Especially since Robin seems to be havin' a good time. I owe that to you. I'd call the evening a success, wouldn't you?"

"As long as you're satisfied, that's what counts," Mariah evaded, gathering up her purse and organizer, suddenly wanting to be alone with her thoughts.

But that wasn't to be. "Wait. I'll see you to your car."

Mariah preceded him out the door and found herself somewhat soothed by the cool, damp air. It had rained that day, but now the sky was clear and deep, with a full-faced moon, regally sedate, peering down at them between the treetops. The silver white stars were more effusive, millions of flickering candle flames.

Here was harmony, in this setting. Simple, real—and appealing to her on the most basic of levels.

Something cold and wet touched her fingertips. Even realizing it was only Lucy's nose, Mariah was startled, jerking her hand away and stumbling on the porch step.

Jeb was there to steady her with a hand under her elbow, and the warmth of his touch renewed her confusion. She moved away from him, the turf soft under the soles of her shoes as she crossed to her car.

Once there, though, she didn't open its door.

"Is something wrong, Mariah?" Jeb asked from behind her.

She shook her head. "No, not really. Except...it just

doesn't seem to me that this party brings us that much closer to reaching your objective of making more of a lady out of Robin.''

"Well, sure, I guess that's true, but it's helped her on another front, I think. It's good for her to feel this is her home, that she can ask her friends over when she wants. To know neither me or Wiley are likely to head for the hills at the sight of a bunch of girls in the living room or feminine decorations around the house.''

She thought him perceptive to have recognized that development. But she wondered if he had grasped the one she'd observed, the concern uncle and niece had for each other that, for better or worse, seemed to precede their own wants and needs.

Before she could broach the matter, Jeb continued, "Which sort of brings up something I've been meanin' to talk to you about.''

She turned to find him standing a few feet away, fingers jammed into the front pockets of his jeans, strong features set into relief by the dim illumination from the porch light. "Yes?''

"Y'see, more than demonstrating to Robin she's got a home with me and Wiley, or trying to make a lady out of her, I want to be there for her...for all of her needs.'' He cleared his throat, gaze fixed on some point past her shoulder. She realized now that she'd drawn herself out of her self-absorbed funk, that he had seemed a bit preoccupied, too. Once again she privately reprimanded herself for losing perspective. She was on the job this evening and should be focusing on her client—and what his needs were.

"Yes?'' Mariah prompted again.

"It's just that tonight when I saw her in that new outfit we bought, with her hair pulled up in one of those fancy braids, I was near to bowled over by how grown-up she looked. And I'm not such an ignorant yahoo I can't see it's like to be real soon the boys'll start noticin' her, too, and

I don't want *her* to be totally ignorant about...you know—"

With a huff of impatience, he turned his head to the side, fingers still crammed into his front jeans pockets and shoulders hunched. Then he shrugged, almost a conscious easing of the tension in his shoulders. His jaw steeled, as if he girded his nerve.

"About sex," he said bluntly.

"Oh! Of course." Mariah could have cursed the heat that rose to her cheeks, not from embarrassment so much as annoyance with herself. She should have anticipated the need to cover such matters with Robin and brought it up to Jeb herself. So why hadn't she?

"You're absolutely right," she responded in her most businesslike tone, "I'd be more than happy to research and make recommendations on which books deal best with the topic. I wouldn't be surprised if there were even some specifically geared at educating the developing adolescent—"

"I'm not talkin' just about the mechanics or differences in plumbing." His gaze pinned hers, now direct and unfaltering. "Sure, I want to prepare her as much as possible for the changes she's going to be experiencin', but I want to let her know she can come to me with all her questions and whatever problems she might come up against, both physically...and emotionally."

Again his jaw tensed, though this time it seemed as if to suppress a secret pain. "I just don't want her to get hurt, Mariah. I know I've got a lot to learn, but I won't let Robin down on that score."

He really was admirable, this simple man with his simple dream of creating a haven of security for his niece. How to tell him, though, that he was essentially wrong to do so, for Mariah knew from personal experience the downside of such a sheltered existence. She herself had been raised in a relatively isolated environment, having attended private girls' schools most of her life, going from the security of home into marriage, never really getting a chance to discover what the real world was like until adulthood.

She leaned a hip against the car door, hugging her organizer to her chest as she tried to decide how to approach the subject.

"Your determination is commendable, Jeb, and I'll help you as much as I can to achieve your aim. But I'm afraid as badly you want to protect Robin, there's only so much you can—or should—do."

Blue eyes glinted contentiously at that. "You mean because I'm a backwater rube raised without a clue as to what makes a woman tick?"

"No!" she automatically denied, then gave an impatient sigh. They'd never get anywhere if they got defensive with each other again. But she felt very strongly that Jeb had to understand the distinction she was trying to make. "I mean there are simply some rites of life no one will be able to prepare Robin for or protect her against, which is what I think you're talking about. Like falling in love—and having her heart broken."

The long, lonesome moan of a train whistle sounded in the distance. This conversation was getting into territory she wasn't ready to explore, even in her own mind. So once again Mariah fell back on her professional persona—or more accurately, her upbringing—as she went on formally, "My recommendation would be to ask one of Robin's female teachers, whom she likes and trusts, to go over the birds and bees with Robin, establish a rapport and an open line of communication. But it should definitely be a woman with whom she has the likelihood of having a long-term relationship, as either a mentor or a mother figure."

Yes, Mariah thought, she was here to do a specific job, and that only. She wouldn't have the opportunity to watch Robin spread her wings and take to glorious flight as she explored the world, wouldn't be here to console her, woman to woman, when she fell back to earth, bruised and hurting.

Could she fault Jeb for wanting to protect Robin from that?

Jeb set one fist against the doorjamb, near her shoulder. "Are you suggesting Robin might be better off with Anita, Lisa's sister? Because I'm not willin' to give up on lookin' after Robin's welfare—not yet."

"No, but there is something that you can do because of who *you* are to Robin. You have a wonderful opportunity to instill in her a self-esteem she'll be able to take with her into her adult relationships. You can teach her how special she is, deserving of a man's utmost respect. That she should accept no less, should never be made to feel lacking for being herself, whatever that may be—"

Mariah paused, realizing she'd once again spoken revealingly and perhaps unwisely. But she couldn't be sorry, for voicing such thoughts helped her get a handle on her own feelings about Stephen and what had gone wrong—or perhaps had never been right—in their relationship.

She stared at that large hand, clenched against the side of her car. It looked incapable of even attempting so fine a task as braiding a girl's hair, yet he'd evinced no reluctance at trying—of doing his utter best to understand and meet her needs.

For half a second, Mariah experienced a sharp stab of jealousy. Still, she couldn't prevent herself from laying her hand over Jeb's to emphasize her next words. "In fact, I can't think of anyone better qualified to teach her such an attitude than you. By example, you can help her establish her standards and teach her to be true to them always, never let them slip for even an instant...."

Her voice trailed off as she was distracted by the change in Jeb's expression. Strangely he looked almost...angry.

"So you think I set quite an example?" he asked.

Mariah shook her head at his inflection. "Of course. That's what I just said. Because you—"

"I can teach her not to be lured into any relationship that's even one inch beneath her *standards*." He was staring pointedly at her hand as it lay over his.

She dropped it, confused—and experiencing a distinct rise of that inner turmoil she'd dealt with earlier.

"But, of course," Jeb went on in that lazy, tangibly sensual accent, "how's she supposed to know what she wants—or doesn't want—until she tests the waters?"

"W-what's that supposed to mean?"

His lashes flickered as his gaze fell to her mouth, and all thoughts of their conversation flew from her head as it hit her: he wanted to kiss her!

Mariah pressed back against the car, somewhat in alarm, but it could have just as easily been in invitation. For Jeb's answer was to prop his other hand near her opposite shoulder, going toe-to-toe with her, virtually the same way he had boxed her in as they'd sat at that tiny table at that bar in Denison. As with that time, Mariah again felt Jeb had followed her out here for reasons having more to do with something other than his niece. A stirring of pleasure expanded in her chest at the possibility that he might feel tempted to lure her to him, that he might find her so compelling he couldn't resist the opportunity to steal a kiss from her....

And so she would let him kiss her—for reasons having very little to do with helping him or Robin.

Mariah drew a shuddering breath, on a crest of anticipation as, elbows unlocking, arms slowly bending, chin dropping, Jeb leaned toward her, leaned into her.

Then his mouth touched hers, a cool, light pressure at first that took no time to grow warm and firm, then hot and hard as Jeb kissed her ardently. And Mariah kissed him back with as much fervor, drinking in the taste of him, tangy and savory. Drawing in drafts of air to inhale the scent of him, that of soap and red-blooded male. The ends of his hair brushed against her cheekbone in a tickling caress. The weight of him was exquisite, muscular thighs flattened against hers, belt buckle pressing into her belly, making her yearn for him even more.

He was a devastatingly good kisser, not a lot of technique and a whole lot of honest-to-goodness zeal.

His groan of impatience made her realize her bulky organizer, clutched in her arms, was the only obstruction that kept them from fully molding body to body. Lips never losing contact with hers, Jeb reached between them, tugged the notebook from her grasp and tossed it onto the hood of her car as if it were nothing but a sheet of paper. As if it didn't contain all the tangible workings of her business, Saved by the Belle.

Even as Mariah sank her fingers into Jeb's hair and dragged him closer, bringing them the contact they both sought, his action nagged her. *Saved by the Belle.* Jeb had chided her for calling herself so, for believing she could sell a personal philosophy. But the service she provided *wasn't* tangible or all that definable by its very nature. Not like his business, where it was pretty clear-cut as to what the customer could expect to derive from his expertise. Not like *his* nature, which was so very tangible, real and earthy and so, so seductive, making her want to give in to the persuasion, to the physical need—

A need Stephen had said she'd never understand. And one she realized now she'd subconsciously vowed she would never validate.

With a strangled cry of denial, Mariah broke the kiss and struggled within Jeb's embrace, trying to ignore with all her might the seemingly genuine reluctance with which he let her go. She felt a real fear she'd throw herself back into his arms if she dwelt upon it at all.

"I need...I need to go," she choked out.

Mariah groped for the door handle, wrenched it open and

escaped into her car. Too late, she remembered her date
book. The blasted thing still lay on the hood of her car.
She was tempted to leave it, let it slide off at the first turn
and disappear into the bushes while she sped off into the
night.

Apparently Jeb saw the direction of her gaze, for he
reached for the organizer, wiping away any moisture on it
with a swipe along the thigh of his jeans, then handed it to
her through the car window, his expression guarded but
watchful.

She was reminded of when he had performed a similar
gesture, the afternoon she'd met him. Reminded, too, of
that same look of skepticism. But he had sought *her* out,
practically pleaded with her to teach his niece to be a lady.
To teach him how to meet the needs of one.

Thoroughly confused, Mariah took refuge in her proper
persona. "I'll be back at three on Tuesday, as usual, for
Robin's lesson. Until then…good evening."

Without waiting for a reply, Mariah started her car and
pulled away.

However, she could have sworn she heard Jeb drawl,
"Y'all come back now, y'hear?"

Not exactly understated, it was sarcasm nonetheless.

So she could inspire that in men, if nothing else.

Jeb didn't wait for Mariah's taillights to disappear in the
darkness with him gazing after her, moony and calf-eyed.
No way, not this time.

He pivoted on his heel and, with a whistle to Lucy, escaped to the dock, shoes echoing loudly on the boards as
he made a production out of checking over his boat and
making sure his gear was all set for tomorrow's fishing
party, knowing he was acting not much more resolutely. At
least he wasn't hopping in his truck and chasing after Mariah to apologize or worse, to say it was all his fault, that it
was him.

Oh, no *way* was he going to get drawn into that trap!

Too bad he hadn't been able to resist his other impulse, the one to walk her to her car and have a moment alone with her. But he'd been so captivated by her this evening— more than just by her tucked-in waist or the curve of her cheek or her womanly way of moving that whispered, called to him constantly. Rather, he'd been lured in by her care and concern that Robin have a happy birthday, her attention to the girl's particular desires.

He'd been drawn in most of all by the look in her brown eyes when he had made her laugh. It made him feel as if he did have something to offer her besides a passing thrill to satisfy the curiosity he'd seen in there—a look he'd seen before, a long time ago.

He came to the conclusion then that there were just some women who found men of his ilk irresistible, from a purely carnal standpoint. That fascination with a construction worker, mechanic or handyman with a can-do attitude, who knew his way around a barn or a toolbox or any number of vehicles. Or a woman. Someone who could be counted on to wash her windows, then clean her clock, jump-start her car and get her motor going. No excuses. Service with a smile, and no messy complications.

But Jeb had wanted to go a little deeper with Mariah. Wanted to get into that uncharted territory, at least for him, of exploring the female mind and what a woman wanted, emotionally. And what had happened? She'd spelled out how he could best help Robin by demonstrating to her the kind of man who was beneath her standards, standards his niece should never be tempted to let slip. And as Jeb had guessed from her fervent tone, Mariah had once made that mistake in the past—or was determined not to in the future.

And genius that he was, he'd countered that argument by kissing her.

With an oath of self-censure, Jeb hopped back onto the dock, where he sat, feet dangling above the water, arms braced on either side of him. Lucy's claws clicked on the wood as she padded over, her back end doing its usual shimmy in counterpoint to the swish of her tail. She leaned chummily into him, trying to give his face a consoling lick. A pungent odor reached his nostrils.

"Hoo-ey, what have you been rolling in, girl?" he asked as he raised a forearm to foil the main thrust of her affections. He didn't know how Lucy managed to do it, but sometimes she stank to clear your sinuses. "You are gettin' a bath first thing tomorrow morning."

But what would he do tonight? He sure wasn't ready to go back into that trailer and face Robin and the evidence of how futile was his aim to prove to Anita Babcock he could raise his niece according to any standards Anita cared to set, even if he was certain he could never prove to her he was no backward yokel.

What had really hit him in the gut this evening, seeing Robin with her hair up, was how much like Lisa—and Anita—the girl had looked. And he realized how Robin was always going to miss out on half of her background, half of her upbringing, no matter who was given custody of her. It was important Robin grow up with a sense of both her mother's and father's background. He believed that, because he'd been there himself.

Jeb had never had a problem keeping his father alive in his mind. He saw flashes of him every day in Wiley, as he imagined Robin saw her own dad in himself. But his mother—she was completely gone to him now, likely because there had never been a replacement for her to whom he might have transferred such tender feelings. He hadn't even the example of a mother in his own life to give him a handle on how to deal with Robin.

It made him wonder if the girl *might* not be better off with her aunt.

Resistance and denial rose in his throat like bitter bile, which in turn made him wonder whether his innermost intent really was to see to his niece's best interests. Or could it be this whole educating of Robin stemmed from something much less noble—something personal between him and Anita?

Jeb tipped his head back and stared up at the sky, remembering.

He had met her at Cody and Lisa's wedding, when he'd been his brother's best man, Anita her half sister's maid of honor. The attraction had been immediate and strong, though nothing had come of it but some flirting. Then a year later, when he was seventeen, Jeb had gone down to College Station to visit Cody, who'd been in his last year of grad school. It had been one of those weekends set up for high-school students to spend time checking out the campus to see if they might attend A&M. Cody had wanted him to consider college an option, but even then Jeb had known he'd already found his calling. Still, he'd been willing to take a look, especially since he was able to spend time with his revered older brother and new wife. And with Anita, then a freshman at the university.

That was when lightning had struck. He'd fallen one hundred percent in love with the girl.

Over the course of the next few months, he visited Cody and Lisa every chance he got. But he came to see Anita. She was the first woman he'd gone to bed with, and Jeb hadn't minded admitting it felt good to know she wanted him, too. Heck, it puffed him up like a rooster with a full henhouse. He saw how it was with Cody, how proud he was to have caught a lady like Lisa. Well, little brother wasn't doing too badly for himself, either.

And so after he graduated high school, Jeb had asked Anita to marry him. He'd wait for her, till after she finished her schooling. He knew he had little materially to offer a woman used to finer things, but he loved her with all his heart, would always work hard to make her happy. Neither would their children want for what mattered most; wherever they went in this world, they'd have a strong foundation of love and solid values to build their own lives upon.

Her reaction had been less than enthusiastic. No, he'd answered her question, he wouldn't be following in his brother's footsteps into college and grad school. He was a fishing guide. His heart and home were on Texoma.

That's when she told him he was crazy to even dream she might live in a trailer out on a lake with him and his uncle, be a barefoot fishwife to his Bubba J. Then, while he stood there glass-eyed and slack-jawed in shock—probably looking exactly like the fish she disparaged—Anita declared she had never really cared for him, had only found him an interesting diversion, a little redneckin' recreation.

Closing his eyes, Jeb shut out the night, tried to shut out the memory of that humiliating conversation. He'd been cut to the bone. He never told Cody, never asked what Anita had told him and Lisa, and they apparently thought it in the best interest of the future of all their in-laws to leave well enough alone. Jeb had never told Wiley, either, even if he knew his uncle had somehow gleaned the gist of the situation. Otherwise, Jeb was certain, Wiley wouldn't have dangled Mariah in front of him.

And damn if he hadn't risen to the bait.

But there had been Mariah's words of judgment, then her surrender under his touch before her rejection of him when she'd shoved him away. And that made him sure as God made green apples she didn't feel the same sort of intense, complex feelings for him as he was beginning to feel for her.

Pensively he rubbed the edge of one thumb across his lower lip, remembering the feel of her soft, full mouth under his, how she'd urged him close, to take the kiss deeper. In that instant, he'd gotten the briefest of impressions that he *had* touched her heart and satisfied some need in her—both physically and emotionally.

And temporarily—just like with Anita?

"Yeah, right," he muttered aloud. Still, his footfall was not quite so heavy as he walked back to the trailer, Lucy at his heels with the usual incorrigible spring in her step. Because tonight, Jeb knew, he'd thrown out a few tempting tidbits of food for thought of his own.

Now all there was to do was sit back and wait to see what was biting.

Platter Flats. He'd first taken Mariah up to
to get her a license, still wondering what her
He in no way believed it had to do with her
learn to fish. But he would bide his time. Two
his game.

, there'd been Wiley to get past. He had said
han "Givin' Texoma a try after all, are you,
he filled out the form, but his facial expression
es. Jeb only hoped no one else noticed, though
ve it away himself in reaction to his uncle's
w, you jest be sure to take your cues from Jeb,
your best bet for catchin' yourself a big 'un.''
couldn't be sorry to be put in this situation,
reason. He'd wanted the opportunity to show
tuff, and now he had it.

-practiced ease, he steered the boat along the
drop-off until he saw what he needed to on the
. Cutting the motor, he let the boat glide to a
utting the anchor down slowly, barely raising
he water, the bow of the boat pointing into the
pot had one of the best shallow water–deep
ations on the lake, making it a good place to
ut any time of day. It was also really pretty,
w in mid-May, when the foliage along the
ll the new, paler green of spring. A familiar
carried in on the breeze, at once ripe and fresh.
-afternoon sun glancing off the surrounding
ne bluffs, the water looked pure sapphire, a
on for the cloudless dome above. Blue skies
ls usually made for lackluster striper fishing;
Jeb's favorite kind of day out on the lake.
" he said as he selected a rod from the rack
r, "let's see if we can teach this landlubber
ule, Robin?"
ur fish and its druthers," his niece obligingly
n her perch on the edge of the boat, arms

Chapter Six

Mariah could tell something was wrong the moment she
pulled up next to the mobile home. Jeb had come out to
the porch upon seeing her car turn into the driveway. His
jaw was set, hands crammed into the front pockets of his
faded jeans, the brightness of his blue eyes similarly
washed-out. Robin, who normally greeted her, was no-
where in sight.

"What's up?" Mariah asked, stepping out of the car.

Jeb jerked his head toward the trailer behind him. "She's
decided she doesn't want to be a part of this plan of ours."

"How so?"

"She said nothing's any fun anymore. The piano lessons
are boring. She'd rather read comic books than the classics
you recommended for her. She refuses to wear any of her
new clothes because she'll just get 'em all 'skanky,' she
says, the first time she plays with Lucy. Oh, and that barrette set you gave her for her birthday? I found it in the
waste can. When I asked her about it, she said she'd just
as soon cut off all her hair if it meant she wouldn't have
to look at another hair doodad in her life. Not only that,

she follows me and Wiley around like a puppy, grills us on what went on while she was at school, like we're hiding something from her.''

He ran a hand through his own unruly strands, clearly frustrated. "I hope to heaven you know what's goin' on, 'cause it's way beyond me.'' He gave her a desperate look. "It's two weeks till the social worker comes out to do the home study. Is it me, something I'm doing or not doing?''

From a nearby tree branch, a squirrel chattered, bottle-brush tail switching madly, and heralded Lucy's approach.

"Oh, I don't think it's you, Jeb.'' She chose to ward off the dog's exuberant greeting rather than climb the porch steps in retreat, not wanting to get too close to Jeb lest she reach out in comfort as she had before—and set off the yearning in her that had nothing to do with her purpose here.

It had been almost two weeks since that incident, and in the ensuing time Mariah had worked doubly hard to achieve results with Robin, believing the progress they made must be tangible in order to measure its value. Yet now it seemed, in her search for validation, she had once again overlooked what should be her real focus.

She concentrated, trying to think as an eleven-year-old girl would think. Or how a woman would feel being forced to change herself—as if how she had been before wasn't good enough.

"I think," she finally said, "that Robin must be reacting to what we're doing to her, overwhelming her, giving her a crash course on everything, making changes to her world left and right, till she doesn't know which end is up." She smiled ruefully. "I bet nothing *is* any fun anymore."

"Well, she's not the only one feelin' that way," Jeb grumbled. "Here I am practically handin' her every privilege a girl could want on a silver platter, and she's turning her contrary little nose up at 'em.''

"Welcome to female adolescence," Mariah murmured,

and Jeb slanted her a penetrati
to one of his unwilling, uneve
knowledging. It was the first s
days, and it sent a bona fide sh

Quickly she turned away fro

"So what's our next step wi

Resting her chin on the edg
narrowed her eyes in thought, a
with that sleek-looking boat be
it.

"I've got an idea. Why don
taking me out for a fishing le
along.''

"A fishing lesson?" he parro
hind her. "But I thought we w
her away from that sort of a
know, girl-type things.''

Eyebrow cocked, Mariah loo
der. "Girls can become practic
as every one of us can do w
minds to doing.''

She'd purposely and perhap
the questions she'd posed to F
the girl and her uncle. And as t
context broader than just that c
of Jeb's, including her own ne
as well.

She simply couldn't find anyt
for all of them.

Jeb studied her with his usu
ously leery of her purpose. Yet s
for when he murmured an offha
the flame in his blue eyes made
bitten off more than she could

Forty-five minutes later Jeb
Lucy were motoring past Littl

way out
Bubba J.':
plan was.
wanting to
could play

Of cour
little more
Mariah?"
spoke volu
he nearly
parting, "
Mariah. H

Still, Je
whatever
Mariah hi

With lo
edge of th
sonar scre
stop befor
a dimple i
wind. Thi
water com
fish just a
especially
bank was
loamy sm
With the
white lim
fitting ref
and low v
still, this

"All ri
near the r
to fish. Fi

"Know
answered

hooked around Lucy's neck. A bright orange life jacket, required by law for children under twelve, engulfed her torso, making those arms and her legs look even longer and thinner.

"What's that mean?" Mariah asked. She was seated on one of the three bolted-down chairs and looked reluctant to try standing yet, given the slight rolling of the boat.

"It means number one, you got to know what stripers prey on, that being gizzard shad." Jeb flipped open the live-well and scooped out one of the wriggling, silvery baitfish he'd pulled from Bubba J.'s tank when they'd bought Mariah's license. He hooked the shad expertly, talking as he did so. "Then you need to know where the stripers are likely to be, both seasonally and on an everyday basis. See, this isn't a real prime time to fish, *that* being the cooler, early-morning hours, because the fish are most active and hungry then, preferring to lay low during the hot of the day. But this flat is just up from the river channel. More like to be activity goin' on from a vertical standpoint."

He handed the rod to Mariah, who took it gingerly and stood, bracing herself against the edge of the seat. He wondered for the tenth time what her plan was today—if there even was a plan.

"You sure you're up to this?" he asked.

That brought a spark leaping to her brown eyes. "Yes."

"Fine, then. You'll have more balance and control if you set a wide stance and try to lean a little forward on the balls of your feet."

He wished he'd thought to offer her a pair of shorts and a T-shirt from the lost-and-found box back in the boat house, rather than have her risk her nice clothes getting dirty. At least he had an extra gimme cap, a green one that sat on her head like a too-big bowl. Her cinnamon-colored hair trailed down her back, and made her look as young as Robin. Or would have if it hadn't been for the expanse of feminine leg showing beneath her above-the-knee split skirt. It was the first time he'd gotten a good look at her legs, and they were as shapely as the rest of her figure. And creamy pale. She would burn in an instant.

He stooped to flip open a storage compartment. "Here, you better put on some of this sunblock first."

"Oh, yes." She glanced down at herself. "Good thinking."

Good thinking but bad move, Jeb thought. Because as a result he had to stand there, holding her rod for her, and watch her smooth the lotion over those legs. It was only when his gaze had wandered a few feet higher that he realized he'd been staring—and Mariah had noticed.

With an adjusting tug on the bill of his cap and another glance at the sonar, he directed, "We're going to go around ten pulls down. Push the button there to release the reel, pull out about ten arm lengths, then turn the handle back to lock the reel."

Awkwardly she struggled to comply and almost dropped the rod into the water. He knew he could have helped her with his hand over hers from behind, but he wasn't going to use that obvious ploy to get close to a woman. Although, he wondered if the snare had already been set, with him jumping on the opportunity to teach her to fish.

Or had he trapped himself by letting her into his world where she could see what he was really like, and perhaps pass judgment upon him?

"I know what. Robin, why don't you grab a rod and show Mariah what I mean."

Robin hopped to, and soon the two of them had their bait down in the stripers' strike zone, even if Mariah still looked as awkward as...well, as a Southern belle on a fishing expedition. "Hold the rod with both hands, one in front of the reel and one behind it. Keep the rod tip 'round belly-button high. And for pete's sake, don't stand there flat-footed or you could be in for a surprise."

"What do you mean?" Mariah asked.

"I mean stripers don't mess around with the bait like other fish might. They get it and go. And they'd just as soon take hook, line and sinker with them."

Determinedly Mariah gripped the rod and struck a stance, looking like some erstwhile Captain Ahab. And a good thing, too. No sooner had she done so than the rod tip jerked down to the water. She gave a yelp of surprise.

"Set the hook," Jeb instructed before seeing the blank look on Mariah's face. In a flash, he was behind and reaching around her, despite his resolve not to, his fingers closing over hers to jerk back on the rod with all his might. "Keep the rod tip up. There you go, girl, now crank him in. Feels like you got yourself somethin' braggin' size."

"Already? But I just started fishing." Mariah braced the butt of the rod against her stomach and turned the handle on the reel. Within seconds a two-foot-long fish came splashing out of the water, its silver sides flashing in the sun as its tail flicked back and forth furiously.

Grabbing the long-handled landing net, Jeb set a hand on Mariah's rod to drop the striper back into the water to capture it. He caught its lower jaw between his thumb and forefinger and clamped down, which stopped the striper from flopping around and hurting itself. With the ease of years of practice, he swiftly pulled his needle-nosed pliers from his back pocket and removed the hook from the striper's lip.

"Yee-haw!" He held it up, grinning. "No record breaker, but I'd guess he's a good fifteen, sixteen pounds."

Mariah stared at her quarry. "That was so…easy. That's all it takes to catch a fish?"

Jeb felt the smile fade from his face, disappointment and self-reproof for that disappointment slicing through him. He had wanted to show off his expertise to her, and now he had. Where had he gotten the insane idea she'd be impressed by him demonstrating the finer points of his trade?

Before he could respond to Mariah, Robin spoke up.

"Sure, that's all it takes—if you've got my uncle Jeb bringing you to the place where the fish'll be biting. And selecting the right tackle and baiting your hook the right way by hookin' the shad through both lips so it'd swim down to where the stripers were suspended, and helping you set your hook so the fish didn't get away."

All this was said respectfully by Robin, with only a hint of gentle reproof. Jeb's bruised ego was somewhat revived. He wasn't one to encourage truancy, but in his book, the girl had just earned herself a little "gone fishin'" time from her lessons.

"I see," Mariah murmured, switching her thoughtful gaze from the girl to him, much as Jeb had seen her do that first afternoon they'd met. "I didn't mean to...dismiss the years of knowledge and skill involved in bringing this fish in. I'm sorry, Jeb."

He shrugged, busying himself with getting the striper packed in the ice chest. "It's no big deal."

Then he heard her ask shyly, "I'd like to try again, if I may."

He glanced up at her probingly, and he saw the sincerity in her gaze. For a moment he wondered if she meant more than just taking another stab at fishing.

"I suppose I could show you how to work with a jerk bait for a while," he suggested. "Top-water fishing with a lure takes a little more technique than fishing with live bait."

He set her rig up again, this time with a pencil popper. After a fifteen-minute lesson in flipping and jerking her lure, Jeb let Mariah be. The only way to get the hang of it was to keep practicing.

Even with the breeze, it quickly grew hot. A red-tailed hawk spiraled over the treetops farther up the shoreline, its rusty brown wings outstretched and cupping the wind beneath them. Of habit, Jeb reached back over his shoulders, grasped two handfuls of T-shirt and pulled it over his head.

He had tossed it on one of the seats before noticing how Mariah now ogled him.

She whipped her attention back to her business.

Yes, two could play this game. Hiding a smile, he grabbed the sunblock and started spreading it over his arms and chest, not altogether necessarily, given the tan base he'd already started. "Okay, what's the second rule of fishing, Robin?"

"Concentrate," the girl piped up, "concentrate and, oh yes, concentrate."

She tossed him a sassy grin; of course, he had pretty much made a litany of that point.

"That's right. Got that, Mariah?"

Mariah, to his pleasure, gave him a mock salute of good-natured acknowledgment.

Jeb grinned back with the same goodwill. And with thanks. He had no idea how she had known what to do to turn Robin's attitude around, but he was grateful to her. His niece was being a model of cooperation and helpfulness, showing Mariah how to present and retrieve her lure. He could barely believe this was the same girl who, not two hours ago, had stuck out her chin and rejected their efforts to make a lady out of her—and had made him almost chuck this whole plan himself.

If it had just been a fit of rebellion or even disobedience, Jeb could have handled the situation. What had scared the heck out of him, though, was how Robin had looked the spitting image of Anita, distant and proud, pronouncing judgment.

The very last thing he wanted was for her to become a little snob! Surely there was a way to keep her from turning into one while still acquiring the qualities he'd recognized Lisa as having: graciousness, thoughtfulness, a certain quiet strength and wisdom and integrity.

Or were they the kind of qualities he saw in Mariah?

He came out of his musing as Mariah asked, "So what

was it like for you and your brother growing up here on Texoma?''

He wondered again at her motives, but answered accommodatingly enough. ''Of course, it was a great way to grow up, especially for two boys. We were like Tom Sawyer and Huck Finn, only we didn't have to play hooky to go fishin'. It was our *business* to know what was biting and where. Sheer heaven to a little boy. At least, it was to me.''

''What about Dad?'' Robin asked.

Jeb propped a sneaker-clad foot on the edge of the boat, leaning a forearm on the stainless-steel horizontal brace across the top of the control panel and checking the sonar screen as he did so to make sure they were still over that school of fish. ''Cody, I think, wasn't quite so interested in the actual fishing part as he was the mechanics of the equipment and tackle. He'd take apart a reel and study the physics of how it worked, or he'd tinker with the boat or down-rigger.''

''What's a down-rigger?'' Mariah asked, now dutifully keeping her attention on her fishing, lower lip caught between her teeth. Jeb couldn't help but be drawn to her.

''A down-rigger's that reel to your left with the cable on it.'' He pointed. ''You use it when you're fishin' at precise depths to take your lure down to the striper's strike zone. They're expensive but near to a necessity, like a good sonic-wave sonar system is, in the hot summer months when the fish're lolling around in deeper, cooler waters. That was why Wiley finally forbade Cody to go near the one on his old boat, after havin' to replace a 'rigger Cody'd messed up so bad it couldn't be fixed.'' Shaking his head, Jeb chuckled. ''And I'm sure that's why Cody became an engineer. To get paid to disassemble stuff and figure out a better way to make it work. It was definitely his calling.''

''So did you and Dad get into the kind of trouble Huck and Tom did?'' This question came from Robin.

''Ooh, yeah.'' Jeb chuckled again. '''Course, out here,

you didn't have to go lookin' for trouble, even though we found our share. It'd often come right to you.''

"Like what?"

Jeb had already noticed Robin's rapt expression, her rod all but forgotten in her hands. Suddenly he wanted badly to bring his own brand of influence to her upbringing.

"You know that bois d'arc up by Bubba J.'s? Well, it just seemed strange to your dad that here were all these osage oranges," he said, referring to the tree's green, soft-ball-sized fruit, "and not a single use for them. You couldn't eat 'em or feed 'em to livestock or use 'em for barbecue fuel like you can mesquite. Nothing. So one summer, Cody decided our project would be to make a list. 'One Hundred and One Uses for Horseapples.'''

Robin abandoned any pretense of fishing now, replacing her rod in the rack and taking a seat on the edge of the boat near the cockpit. "How far did you get?"

Jeb scratched his eyebrow. "At first, nowhere. Every day for a month, Cody and I'd think on it, and we were gettin' pretty desperate when Cody hit on an idea. It didn't take long after that to get our quota of uses, but the gist of each one was a different surface an osage orange could be smashed against. You had your horseapple-smash-against-a-tree-trunk use—" he ticked them off on his fingers "—your horseapple-smash-against-asphalt use. Or brick walls, or fence posts, or the Dempsey Dumpster. Oh, it got so we were on a roll, except my coordination and aim weren't as good as Cody's. The day came when I threw a big old warty osage orange right through the back window of Bubba J.'s."

Remembering the incident, he full-out laughed this time. "Did Wiley *yell* at us. Yep, that was good for a trip down to the boat house for both of us, where we got a couple hours apiece of private thinking time."

"Why'd Dad get punished if you broke the window?"

"That time it was for thinkin' up such a wasteful, pointless game. Most of the time, though, he got it for leadin' me on, and I got it for bein' so gullible. Like the time I had a crush on this little girl at school—''

Just in time, Jeb collected himself. He cleared his throat. ''Shoot, I shouldn't be tellin' you this story.''

''No, tell!'' Robin pleaded, hands clasped between her knees, eyes shining.

''Really, I don't think it's appropriate. I mean, it's nothin' bad. We were just bein' typical boys. But boys of a certain age can be pretty immature and even, uh, kind of crude when it comes to girls.''

He felt himself floundering and could have cursed himself for doing so. Over Robin's head, he glanced at Mariah for support, which she gave in the form of her own question. ''Don't you think it might help a girl of a certain age to know what's going on in the minds of her male peers?''

She raised her delicate eyebrows in response to him lowering his at her. He knew what she was implying, what she had said the evening he'd walked her to her car: how, *because* he was a man, he could instill in Robin a perspective she'd be able to take with her into her adult relationships. Abruptly he saw that statement from his own changed perspective—a positive one instead of the negative one he'd interpreted at the time.

Of course, he could be completely wrong....

He searched her expression for a clue, but all he got back was what seemed to him as a most sincere encouragement in her toffee-colored eyes. He wondered if she knew what she was suggesting. What perspective, really, would be gained not just from Robin learning more about the adolescent male mind—but Mariah learning more of him?

He turned back to Robin, deciding to give it a shot for her sake if no other. ''Y'see, Cody was at that in-between age, old enough he knew he wanted to chase girls but not old enough to know what to do with one if he caught her. A boy spends a whole lot of energy at that age just trying to get the girl he likes to notice him, or he's thinkin' up new ways of devilin' her, in sort of a reverse psychology. Tease the poor girl to death so she and everyone else won't think you like her. I got a fine demonstration of both kinds of behavior one day on the way home from school, when I saw Cody take two of those horseapples and, well—'' Jeb commanded himself not to blush ''—he put 'em in the front of his T-shirt. Then, chest stuck out and hands on his hips, he strutted past the girl he liked and all of her friends.''

"No!" Blushing herself, Robin clapped a hand over her mouth, but her laughter came spilling out anyway.

"The girl, of course, thought he was the most offensive boy she'd ever seen, but Cody was well satisfied with his results. He'd definitely gotten her attention.''

"So what did you do to attract the notice of the little girl *you* liked?" Mariah asked as she tried most conscientiously to pay attention to what her lure was doing, which was jerking and quivering more from the vibration of her amusement than any deliberate manipulation.

A charge of apprehension zipped through him about the rest of the story to come. Then he caught her eye and could see nothing but that sincere interest in her gaze.

Figuring himself in for a penny, in for a pound, Jeb went on, "Well, I got a couple of horseapples, too, and Cody saw me strugglin' to stuff them into my shirt. That's when he told me how to get *all* the girls to notice me.''

"How?" Robin prompted avidly.

"Remember, now, I was six years old. Anyway, I sure enough got a sense of my manly potency the next day when I sent a whole playground worth of shrieking girls runnin' for the opposite fence.'' He paused in true storytelling fashion. "Y'see, I'd waltzed right into the lot of them with an osage orange stuck in my britches. Not the front mind you, which would have been bad enough. No, I'd taken Cody's cue and put it down the back.''

"You mean like you'd..." Robin's eyes widened, then

crinkled at the corners as she burst into laughter. "Uncle Jeb!" She clutched her middle, howling so hard she nearly unseated herself. Mariah, too, had gone off in a peal of her silvery laughter, like delicate bells ringing. It caused his own laughter, as well as something else that felt incredibly good, to bubble upward from deep within his chest. Somehow, he realized, he had stumbled upon a means of accomplishing several aims at once, that of teaching Robin as a parent would, while covering, in a roundabout and certainly unique way, the difficult subject of puberty. But most of all, of making her feel more grounded in a sense of history. Like all children, she clearly loved learning about her parents' childhood, loved the opportunity to picture her father at her own age and realize he had a mischievous side, could be childish and rambunctious. Could yearn for validation.

It occurred to Jeb that he spoke little about either of Robin's parents to the girl. But he saw now how she needed to know that, even after losing his own parents and coming to live in a place where he didn't quite fit in, her father had still found ways to have fun, found his own way to fulfillment, his own way to be…happy.

Robin caught the look he gave her and smiled up at him with her old unaffectedness, pure and natural and unbelievably sweet, causing a lump the size of a golf ball to lodge itself in his throat. Suddenly Jeb wanted to pull her into his arms and hold her tight and never, ever let her go. He wanted with all his heart to keep her as she was now, sweet and innocent. To just…keep her. The custody hearing loomed like a freight train speeding toward him down a track, heading for the moment when he would truly be judged proper, competent. Would be judged enough.

Or improper, incompetent—and not enough at all.

He still felt as ill prepared for that moment as a garter snake in a wrestling match with a raccoon.

"Yeah, I was pretty gullible," he said, now completely serious. "Which I've come to believe isn't necessarily a bad thing. A person who's too trustful gets hurt, but a person gets hard, who's never so. I may be just a redneck fishing guide, but I've learned that much about life.''

"What d'you mean, Uncle Jeb?"

Lucy, recognizing some of the pensiveness in her master's voice, crept over to lean against his leg, silky brown eyes offering comfort. He stroked her head. "I mean you've got to leave yourself exposed to the possibility of not getting what you want in order to have a chance at *gettin'* what you want. Which takes a certain amount of courage, and I guess a certain amount of faith. It's like fishing, in a way. You can go out day after day and never even get a nibble. But nothing's a sure thing, except this— you sure enough won't catch even the smallest of fish if you don't put your line in the water. What if, instead of runnin' away, that little girl on the playground had laughed like you and Mariah did, and thought I was kinda brave for takin' a chance on her?''

What if another girl had taken a chance on him? He thought about Anita, both in the context of the past—his past with her—and the future. Robin's future. So far the girl had somehow managed, even with the knocks she'd taken, to stay innocent and trusting. He wanted more than anything for her to remain so, while still learning to land on her feet when life and love sent her for a loop. And for that, he perhaps was not the best teacher. Look how he'd been sent for a loop himself that he'd obviously yet to completely recover from.

His gaze met Mariah's over the girl's dark blond head.

Look at the fall he was taking right now.

"Just try to be wiser than I was, Robbie," he said softly.

"Don't worry, Uncle Jeb," she answered. She looked pure Cody in the way her eyes dwelt fondly upon him, deep with an understanding of his love and concern for her, and in that moment he believed she *would* make it just fine.

They would both make it, but only so long as they strived to hold themselves open to possibilities.

Then his niece looked even more like his brother as her mouth curled into a mischievous grin. "And you can't be a *real* redneck, Uncle Jeb. You may've put a horseapple down the back of your jeans when you were a kid, but your crack still doesn't show in the back when you sit down."

"I *knew* I shouldn't have told you that story." Jeb reached for his niece's ankle, meaning only to threaten her with a toss overboard. But Robin was a spry little thing, dodging away from him and heading for the safety of the back of the boat, giggling the whole way. The problem was, she had to squeeze past the captain's chair and Mariah to get away. The boat wobbled as she bumped Mariah, who windmilled her free arm to recover her balance. Jeb stuck out a hand to steady her as he grabbed for the edge of the boat at the same time with his other hand, to maintain his own balance as he stumbled over Lucy. But instead of catching hold of Mariah, his limb collided with hers.

Which sent her over the side with a shriek and a splash.

Jeb didn't even stop to think. He dived in after her.

The water was freezing, practically knocking the breath clean out of him, and he imagined it hitting Mariah the same way. He saw a murky shape ahead of him and scissor-kicked over to it. Grasping hold of her waist with both hands, he surfaced.

Jeb flicked his hair out of his eyes to find her handily treading water. He felt like a fool, panicking like that, remembering only now that Mariah had told him she was a strong swimmer when he'd given her the option of wearing a life jacket or not.

"I'm sorry, Mariah," he sputtered through the water sluicing down his face. "I didn't mean to push you overboard. I hope your nice clothes aren't ruined, but I'll pay to replace them if they are."

"No, no, it's my fault. You warned me not to get caught

flat-footed.'' Drops of lake water sparkled on her lashes, making her lids look heavy and her gaze bedroom seductive, sloe-eyed instead of doe-eyed.

In a gesture Jeb found incredibly erotic, she lifted her arms and ran her fingers back through her hair, which raised her chest out of the water. The thin cotton of her blouse had become almost transparent, and he saw clearly outlined beneath it the lacy material of her bra.

He realized he was staring like an adolescent at a ladies' undergarment ad, that he still held her as if he was actually preventing her from going under. He let her go.

Something brushed against his leg, and recalling himself, Jeb submerged again to snatch Mariah's rod before it sank to the bottom and he paid hell trying to recover it. Both their caps were goners, he was afraid.

It was when he came back up again that he noticed she was rather absorbed, too, with the rise and fall of his chest as he bobbed in the water.

He would have relinquished his next five commissions to have been alone with her at that moment.

Then a spray of water hit the back of his head and shoulders, and he swung around to see Lucy paddling over to him, tongue lolling from her grinning mouth.

"I'm sorry, Uncle Jeb," Robin said. "I tried to hold her, but she just couldn't stand missin' out on all the fun."

"She might as well get some exercise—there won't be much fishing this spot the rest of today."

Robin was actually the one who looked as if she was missing out on all the fun. Jeb collared Lucy, spun her around and gave her a shove in Mariah's direction before heading for the boat. Once there, he handed Robin the rod, then, gripping the side rail, he extended his other hand to her. "Give me a boost up, will you?"

Bracing herself, she complied. Or tried to as, giving a mighty tug, Jeb pulled her headfirst into the water.

She came up sputtering and splashing and laughing. "Hey, no fair!"

"Welcome to the real world." Jeb grinned. "I told you not to be too gullible. *And* never to forget the third rule of fishing. Which is?"

"Always be careful in the boat and around the equipment."

They didn't spend much more time in the water. It was too cold, and the sun was setting, causing the air temperature to cool off even more. Jeb climbed aboard first, then hiked Robin up and over the side of the boat. Lucy was next, hauled aboard with both his and the girl's help. Then came Mariah, whom Jeb grasped around the waist for the finishing momentum. He let his hands linger there just a few seconds too long.

The sidelong look she gave him reproved but was no less seductive than the one he caught her giving him in the water.

He started the motor while Robin found a couple of towels to wrap around their shoulders and ward off the chill. Lucy stationed herself on the farthest forward point, bracing her front paws on the rail like a figure on the prow of a ship, black-and-white ears and pink tongue flapping backward in the wind.

"I had a great time today, Jeb."

He turned to find Mariah sitting in the same place Robin had while listening to his stories about his childhood. Mariah had the same sort of pure, natural and unbelievably sweet look on her face. Yes, somehow, some way, and without design, he'd accomplished several aims in one stroke today.

One of those aims had been for Mariah Duncan not only to see him in his element, but also to see him for who and what he was and not merely cast in the mold of a certain kind of man, be it backwoods country boy, or redneck, or even fishing guide. He felt he'd accomplished that goal, but mostly because he had been allowed to see deeper into Mariah's character. She seemed so much a real lady, in the best sense of the word—and in the opposite sense of the image of that sort of woman he'd carried with him for the past fourteen years.

Was *he* being unwise—again? For as Jeb gazed back at Mariah, he found himself returning to a certain fantasy that had grown more distinct as the day had faded.

"I'm glad you had fun," he answered her simply.

"I truly did. And thank you for jumping in to save me."

Like you needed it, he almost snorted, except it felt good to play protector to her gentle miss. Yes, it *was* the essence of that steel-magnolia image that drew him to her, just as he was sure his image was very much a component of what attracted her to him: a good ol' boy, Southern as black-eyed peas on New Year's Day, with that can-do, never-say-die attitude born out of the Alamo and delivered with an uninhibited rebel yell.

For some reason, he didn't mind playing that part right now, either.

Jeb raised his eyebrows. "Now, don't go paintin' me in such a noble light," he drawled. "I wasn't jumpin' in to save you so much as I purely didn't want to lose my best graphite rod."

Mariah laughed as she had earlier, that silvery sound that told him she laughed with him, not at him. And in it Jeb found the most seduction of all.

Chapter Seven

Streamers of violet pink and silver blue were streaking across the amber western sky by the time Jeb had maneuvered the boat into its slip. Mariah just tried to stay out of the way as Robin leapt to the dock and helped guide the boat in, obviously having performed that duty many times before.

Once she was safely on the dock again, Mariah found herself feeling even more superfluous as Jeb and Robin worked against the diminishing light to prepare the boat for tomorrow's party of anglers.

She watched as he hosed out the live-well, crouching so that the muscles of his thighs were clearly molded against his damp jeans. As with her fascination with his chest earlier today, Mariah found herself mesmerized. She recalled how she'd been attracted to him the first day they met, when he'd looked much as he did now: disheveled, his hair wet and tousled and falling around his temples. A little dangerous, a bit wild. And a whole lot tempting.

A mockingbird made catcalls at her from the branch of a nearby cottonwood. Yes, as impressed as she was with his professional abilities, there were probably a few more of Jeb Albright's talents she'd yet to learn to appreciate fully.

Blast her luck if Jeb didn't glance up just then and catch her staring at him. But then, they had been making eyes at each other like this all afternoon. From the moment they'd met, really.

"I should be going," she said not altogether steadily, folding the damp towel she'd worn around her shoulders. "Where would you like this?"

"Keep it for now. It's better than nothing against the nip in the air." His gaze dropped fleetingly to her pale green blouse which, she knew, wasn't quite as transparent as it had been when dripping wet, but was still rather sheer.

Mariah hugged the folded towel to her chest. It didn't offer quite the protection—or security—of her organizer. Or her pearls.

"You're welcome to use the shower at the house," he offered, standing and wiping his hands on the seat of his jeans, "if you were of a mind to clean up before heading out. I'd hate to see you get your car seats musty with lake water."

The playfulness between them that had characterized the afternoon had vanished, and she wasn't entirely easy with the tension that supplanted it. As if, once again, Jeb wanted something more than just to see to her safety or comfort.

"Thank you, but I think I'll pass." She tucked a rather damp lock of hair behind her ear and away from her face. "Besides, what good will cleaning up do me if I've nothing to change into?"

"There's a box of clothes in the boat house," Robin provided helpfully. "I bet I could find something you could wear. And then, I know—you could stay for supper, too!" she went on with a burst of enthusiasm. "Uncle Jeb'll have your striper cleaned and filleted in no time, and I can show you how to make Wiley's special marinade to cook it in. And afterward we can play cribbage. It'll be fun!''

The evening did sound inviting, promising simple pleasures, of which she'd shared so many this afternoon with this man and his niece. She'd been touched, as always, by their obvious desire to see each other happy. And she'd never felt less needed.

"Really, I couldn't intrude," she demurred.

"Sure, you could!" Robin guilelessly countered. Mariah decided then and there the girl *could* use instruction in some of the subtleties of social discourse.

"Robin," Jeb quietly reproved, "maybe Mariah has other obligations. We're not the only clients Saved by the Belle has got right now."

"Oh, but I don't even think about her that way anymore, do you?"

Jeb didn't answer, and for the life of her Mariah didn't have the nerve to look at him. Robin, however, had no such compunction as her perceptive gaze shifted between them. Mariah had wondered how much of the unspoken byplay the girl had picked up on today, and now she knew, for Robin declared, seemingly out of the blue, "I just remembered I haven't practiced my piano today."

Jeb and Mariah watched as she dashed to the trailer. It was as if she'd never thoroughly denounced the instrument and everything having to do with it barely three hours ago.

Jeb shook his head, muttering something that sounded like "women." He turned to her, taking in her hunched shoulders. "You look like you're freezing. Even if you don't have time for a shower, there probably is something that'd fit you in that box. Nothin' fancy, but at least it'd be dry."

She saw the sense in his suggestion. "Well, all right."

He unlocked the boat house and pulled the string to turn the light on, showed her where the box was, then closed the door behind him to let her change in privacy. Mariah couldn't resist taking a look around as she slid out of her clothes.

Like Jeb's boat, the interior of the boat house was neat and orderly and smelled, naturally, of lake water. Several tackle boxes lined the shelves, each labeled cryptically with names like Sassy Shads, Pencil Poppers, Jigs, 20# Triline. One wall was filled with fishing rods all lined up in racks; another had cast nets hung on it. There were a couple of battery chargers and extra boat seats, a workbench she could picture Jeb standing at, engrossed in some task that he pursued with his usual meticulousness.

Yes, all was as ordered and neat as a hospital operating room. Except for one corner where sat a low stool. On it was the pamphlet on hair braiding she had given Robin. Next to the pamphlet lay a hairbrush, a covered hair band around its handle, and next to it a spool of fishing line, several knots in a foot-long length at the end. Just as she had pictured Jeb, Mariah now saw the other half of the scene: Robin, perched on the stool and chattering away to her uncle as she practiced her knots, holding each effort up for him to approve or correct. Or perhaps she practiced her braids, again soliciting his help.

But no—Jeb said she'd done with such foolishness.

"Mariah?" Jeb knocked lightly on the door.

"Yes, I'm almost finished." Actually she'd been snooping. Mariah pawed through the box of clothes and came up with pair of terry-cloth drawstring pants and a knit crop top, which she hurriedly put on. It still felt a little drafty, since she'd also shed her damp underwear, but as Jeb had pointed out, at least both articles of clothing were clean and dry.

She opened the door, nervously smoothing down her hopelessly messy hair and suddenly reminded of how Jeb had looked—and must have felt—the day she'd caught him fresh from a hard day out on the lake. "Yes, I feel much better," she lied.

His gaze flitted over her briefly before he handed her a zippered plastic bag. "I went ahead and cleaned your catch. Bass is best eaten the day you catch it. And you don't need to get fancy with it. Cooked with butter and lemon, it's great."

"Oh, thank you." She took the bag from him and set it on the stack of her wet, folded clothes and shoes. She'd elected to forego wearing them, too. They were distinctly squishy inside.

He stood on the threshold of the boat house, as if it were hers and not his domain being invaded. "I'm the one who owes you all the thanks in the world, Mariah, for knowin' exactly how to handle Robin. I don't know how you knew what to do, but I'm glad you did."

Venus blinked at her from over his shoulder, a bright white pinprick in the purpling sky.

"Actually I was feeling I'd done very little, and certainly not enough to earn the fee you're paying me," she confessed, her hand going unconsciously to her throat. But she hadn't worn her strand of pearls today, for whatever reason. "I simply thought it would help to show Robin that becoming a woman didn't mean you couldn't let your hair down and have fun. You took it from there, made the afternoon the real success."

He shrugged as if to debate that opinion.

She rested one hip against the workbench. "I know you're set on Robin becoming more…oh, I won't say more ladylike, because I think we both know it's a more involved objective than that. But have you considered just going along as you have been?"

He searched her features in the wan illumination of the bare light bulb. "What do you mean?"

"I mean Robin seemed to me when I first met her so much more…happy than she is now. You, too, in some ways. Why not leave well enough alone?"

"I told you, I can't take that chance."

"What chance? I know you're apprehensive about how you'll stack up against this other family and the advantages they have to offer, but you have advantages, too. Don't you think it helped Robin, helped you both, to talk about Cody today—and to talk about some aspects of the birds and bees in your own way? I thought you struck just the right note with her."

And me, she almost added. She wanted to tell him how his homespun stories and simple but profound philosophy had drawn her to him as nothing else could, because it dovetailed with her own conviction—that one must simply try to lead his or her life in the best way possible. Be true to yourself, but remain open to possibilities for growth.

Mariah recalled telling him how different they were, from vastly different backgrounds, yet she'd realized today they were more alike than not. He, too, had grown up in a rather isolated environment, with little interaction with people. With women. She guessed that as a result, he, too, felt he'd been naive and unwise in love at some point in the past—beyond that years-old encounter with the little girl on the playground. Felt he, too—the who and what of his identity that no amount of effort could change—had come up short somewhere along the way.

Except, hearing that story today, Mariah had come to the conclusion that, while Robin might miss out on some of the finer things in life and a certain refinement in her upbringing being raised by her bachelor uncle, Jeb was providing the girl with what mattered most: love, and such love would stand her through the years better than anything Mariah could teach her. With it, Robin would be so much better equipped to handle whatever disappointments came her way.

Yes, Mariah thought, gazing at his chiseled features dusted with day-old stubble, he may be a bit rough on the outside, but as Robin had said, Jeb Albright was not what Mariah would call a real redneck, either.

But this day had already become too much about Jeb and her, rather than Jeb and Robin.

"What's on your mind, Jeb?" she asked softly.

With a deep sigh, he leaned back against the doorjamb, knee bent and one sole braced flat on the wood, fingers crammed in his front pockets. "I guess I'm feeling pretty ambivalent about just what was accomplished today."

"How so?"

His chin dropped to his chest as he dragged a hand through his already rumpled hair. "Well, what struck *me* today," he said with some reluctance, "was how Robin's always going to miss out on half of her background, no matter who she ends up with, me or Anita. And it seemed pretty unfair to her, even if I don't know how to make it any different."

His voice was made rough by his apprehension, as always, that he do his best for his niece. Yes, Mariah thought, he'd wanted something from her this evening: to work on the situation with Robin, which was, after all, what she was here for.

"You make it sound as if whoever doesn't get Robin will never see her again. Surely both you and Anita will have your opportunities to make your individual impressions on the girl."

"I think that's what we're both afraid of—and what the real problem here is. Probably the biggest reason I hired you." His mouth tightened, and she spotted that flash of inner pain she'd seen before.

"Tell me what's wrong, Jeb," she urged softly. "I want to help, however I can."

The cicadas had started their nightly refrain, a resonant treble that nearly drowned out the crickets' song. Finally he said in a low voice, "Y'see, I know Anita Babcock."

"Know her?" Mariah echoed faintly, for some reason struck with a faint sense of foreboding.

He nodded, still not looking at her. "And she knows me.

Not to put too fine a point on it, but she considers me a redneck bachelor, completely unfit to raise her niece." His jaw bulged stubbornly. "Frankly, though, I'm not crazy about the example she'd set Robin, either."

She shook her head in confusion. "What do you mean?"

"I suppose I'm not completely sure, and that's the problem here, too." Finally his gaze met hers, and it was that clear-eyed look of his, at once searching and surrendering, making what he saw through those eyes just as discerning as what was seen by her. "All I can come up with is, I don't want Robin turning out like Anita. Because Anita Babcock's a...a *real* Southern belle."

Stunned by the obvious denunciation in his voice, Mariah sank back against the workbench, unsure of whether she herself had been complimented or insulted, and unsure of which she'd rather have been. "As I am a Southern belle?" she asked.

"No," he quickly denied. He reached out to finger a damp lock of her hair, and he actually smiled. "That's what I'm tryin' to get at. You're not like Anita, Mariah—not at all."

"I see." But she didn't see. Not at all. She recalled Jeb saying he didn't find proper Southern ladies "real riveting." Then it struck her what she must look like, standing there barefoot in a pair of hip-hugging pants and a crop top, which left a significant swatch of her midriff exposed, much like that barroom waitress.

"I *really* must be going," she declared, reaching for her stack of clothes.

Frowning, Jeb dropped his hand. "Mariah, wait. What's wrong?"

"Nothing!" She dropped the slippery plastic bag containing her filleted bass, and when she stooped to pick it up, her waterlogged shoes slid from her grasp, along with the rest of her clothes. She let fly with a juicy oath that would have had Stephen's eyebrows shooting to his hairline in disapproval.

"Yes, there is," Jeb said, dropping to one knee to help her. "Don't go until we've talked this out."

"No!" That was the last thing she wanted, to know which it was—whether he saw her as some uptight, self-righteous priss or...oh, whatever the opposite of that was!

It barely occurred to her that it *could* be neither.

Impatiently she pushed her hair out of her eyes. It felt rather stringy and smelled not unlike the scent wafting from Lucy. "Before I go anywhere, I have *got* to get this rag-mop away from my face!"

Remembering the covered band she'd seen wrapped around the handle of the hairbrush, she crossed to the corner to get it. She intended to skin her hair back into an untidy ponytail, retrieve her belongings and leave, but she'd scarcely lifted her arms when she heard Jeb behind her. "Here, let me help."

"Oh, *please,*" she said on a short laugh. "This is one skill I think I've mastered."

"Then tell me how well I've learned it."

She was too overwrought to protest further, then too disoriented to do so as he took the brush and began working the tangles from her hair. It was a slow, meticulous process, but he showed no impatience, working from the ends of her hair upward. As always, his willingness to do whatever it took to get the job done was her downfall.

It was a slow, sensuous process. Despite herself, Mariah felt her eyelids drift closed as she gave herself up to the purely tactile sensation of it: the tickle of the bristles on her back through the thin knit top; the exquisite, gentle tug as the brush took its first full stroke; the sheer heaven of Jeb's fingers grazing her neck as he lifted the weight of her hair to brush it from underneath.

His touch was so reverent, so worshipful, so respectful, he soothed her pounding heart, as well.

He braided her hair swiftly, surely, expertly. When he was done, Mariah reluctantly opened her eyes, bereft that it was over. She had wanted him to go on and on.

"Th-thank you," she stammered, her voice reedy. She couldn't turn to look at him, not yet.

She ran her fingers down the length of the braid. "It feels like you did a g-great job. For a man, you're very good with your hands, you know."

Too late she realized how her words sounded.

"Girl, you don't know the half of it." His answer in her ear was whisper soft, delivered in that provocative backwoods drawl. For some reason, she loved it when he called her "girl" almost as much as when he said her name.

Which he did in the next instant. "What is it you want, M'riah?"

"W-what do you mean?"

"I think you know." He was so close, his breath disturbed the loose tendrils at her temple. "What is it you want...from me?"

Wordlessly she shook her head, afraid what she wanted—no, *needed*—from him were mutually exclusive, yet somehow equally important to the self-perspective she'd assured Jeb he had within him to nurture in his niece. To be not just understood and accepted—completely—for herself, but respected and loved completely for being so, as well. Anything less would not be...enough.

Abruptly he stepped away from her, as if he took her silence for an answer. As if he considered it a lost cause.

She knew she must say something or he'd walk away.

"I want...I want you to touch me again," she whispered.

A moment of eternity went by. Then his fingers lightly traced the slope of her shoulders. His palms smoothed over her upper arms and down to her fingertips, then they swept up again over the same route to sketch down once again, as if instead of smoothing the tangles from her hair, he was now smoothing them from her body. It was wonderful, but it was not enough.

"Jeb...*please,*" she begged.

His hands stilled. Mariah couldn't move. She was trembling, trembling all over. Afraid of what would come next, afraid she would never know. Her heart stopped and started a hundred times in the space of a few minutes. Then...oh, then she felt him sweep the braid aside, felt his breath on the side of her neck an instant before his lips touched her there, warm and moist and alive. And still it was not enough. Her hand came up almost of its own volition and not altogether gently grasped the back of his head, pulling him more fully against her. His answer was to score her throat with his teeth. Mariah gasped, but the word that made it from her was *"Yessss."*

With a muttered curse, Jeb turned her into his embrace and—not entirely gently—fused her open mouth to his, as if his desire for her had grown beyond the constraints of gentility. And Mariah knew *that* was what she truly needed—and it seemed, as always, that Jeb was willing to do his utter best to meet those needs.

Tongues touched, twined, mated. Hearts thundered, breaths mingled, merged and became one. Dimly Mariah registered that if she wasn't careful, she'd be spending the night picking splinters out of her behind after a rowdy lakeside rendezvous, but couldn't find it in her to care about anything except that Jeb not stop loving her.

He must have sensed that thought somehow, for he lifted her and set her on the edge of the workbench, nestling between her thighs as the kisses went on and on. Emboldened, Mariah explored with her fingers the fine planes and firm surfaces of Jeb's back through his T-shirt. Craving more-complete contact, she plucked at the tail of his shirt. He understood her silent plea and broke their kiss only long enough to tug the T-shirt off and discard it before bringing her flush against him again.

This was heaven, Mariah thought with a surge of pure rapture. Seeking assurance that she had the ability to inspire the same ardor in him, she spread her fingers on his chest, dragging them through the whorls of hair there. She was rewarded with the quickening of his respiration, the renewed intensity with which he immersed them both in the deepest of kisses.

With a low moan of regret, Mariah pulled her lips from his. But she needed air, which in the next instant she was panting for as the nuzzling of Jeb's mouth along her jaw raised goose bumps all up her spine, tingling into her scalp.

She wrapped her arms around him, afraid she'd topple backward if she didn't. He wouldn't have let that happen, she knew; still, he secured her to him, grasping her waist with his large hands on her bare skin. His thumbs caressed the sensitive flesh of her rib cage, their tips mere millimeters from brushing the even more sensitive underswell of her breasts.

The wave of desire that crashed through her was like nothing she'd ever experienced even in her most intimate moments with Stephen.

"Oh, Jeb!" Mariah opened her eyes to find his hot, blue-flamed gaze on her.

"What do you want, Mariah?" he asked her again, shifting his thumbs in the gentlest of strokes. "Just tell me."

She swallowed, hard. "Does it have to be all of one need and nothing of another?" she asked somewhat desperately.

"No. It's whatever you want, however you want it, girl. And however that is, I can love you like that."

His gaze was filled with that earthy honesty that she'd experienced before. How exhilaratingly direct it was, refreshingly uncomplicated. Natural and...primal.

And also as she had before, Mariah felt the same threat to her emotional well-being, for she could see the seduction in that earthiness, could feel the power in so physical a craving or yearning, an almost undeniable need...

A need that Stephen had said she couldn't, even shouldn't, understand. Not the kind of woman she was.

But she did understand now, with Jeb! Or did she? She recalled the look in his eyes when he'd said Anita Babcock was a real Southern belle. He hadn't exactly been paying the woman a compliment. And yet he'd said she, Mariah, was completely unlike the other woman.

So what *did* she want? No, what did she really *need?*

She shook her head in confusion, not realizing how vehemently negative her reaction must have looked until Jeb dropped his hands, his expression going completely neutral.

She hastened to reassure him. "I'm sorry, Jeb. It's not you, really. It's—" *It's me. Me and my unrealistic expectation of thinking I can prove not to Stephen but to myself that there's a man out there who values and respects those qualities that make me who I am—be it Southern belle or proper lady or whatever—and can still love me completely. And believes that I can fulfill him as completely.*

"Oh, it's all so confusing!" she said, more to herself than Jeb. "Maybe it was growing up so sheltered from the real world and never really being out on my own at all, going straight from college into marriage—"

Jeb tugged her chin up so she had no choice but to look into his searching blue eyes. "You were *married?*"

"Yes, for six years, which you'd think would be enough time for two people to learn all there was to know about each other." She felt her nose clogging up; really, she had cried as much as she was going to about this matter. She had to get on with her life. But she needed to understand, too.

Mariah drew in a deep breath, gathering courage as much as her thoughts. "You talked today about being gullible—well, I think I must be the queen of it. I...I don't want to go into the details, but suffice to say it turned out Stephen wasn't the man I believed him to be—just as I know I wasn't all he expected me to be. And I'm still struggling with what it is I *want* to be.''

His lashes flickered in reflection of his own whirling thoughts. "You didn't want to take a chance you could work that out with him?"

She'd always believed she had tried—and yet Mariah saw now that she hadn't. "No. Because I knew he wasn't going to change. And in my heart, I quite honestly didn't believe *I* should," she confessed. "I still don't. I can't...can't be any other way than what's me, no matter what I might want. That's what I meant a few weeks ago when we were talking about Robin and how to help her form a strong self-perception, help her establish her standards and be true to them always, never let them slip for even an instant."

But she'd recognized from the first that Jeb and Robin already had those essential elements to ensure their happiness: love and respect. What really could she teach them both?

Mariah bent her head, unable to face that searching, honest scrutiny of Jeb's as she told him, "I think it would be best if we discontinued Robin's instruction. I told you at the beginning I wasn't sure what real service I could be to either of you, and now—" She cleared the tears from her throat, found she could go on only by taking refuge in her formal demeanor. "Now I'm certain I haven't effected the kinds of changes that would justify further retaining my services."

"You...you don't want to go on?" Jeb asked quietly.

It wasn't clear whether he meant with him or with her lessons with Robin. Either way, the disappointment and discouragement in his voice was obvious. And the hurt. She made herself look him in the eye, owing him that much. "Don't you see? I don't know if I'm helping or hindering Robin—or you. How could I when I'm so doubtful as to the very essence of what I'm trying to impart?"

He scrutinized her, as if by doing so he could discover every other secret in her heart. Finally he nodded, not exactly in satisfaction, but again with that acceptance of the situation she'd seen before.

"Then I guess I'd be next door to a philistine if I didn't thank you kindly for your time and efforts," he drawled in his good-ol'-boy twang, giving her what she feared would be the last of his wry, crooked smiles she would ever see. But she saw the hurt lurking beneath the surface of his lake blue eyes.

He helped her down from the workbench, helped her gather her things, saw her to her car, all with a constrained, gentlemanly reserve she knew was her doing. Except he'd always been a gentleman, in the truest sense of the word. Thoughtful, respectful, with a purpose and integrity that had drawn her to him from the first.

She stopped short of getting into her car, wanting to say something more, something to halt this parting that struck her as so incomplete.

Yet there was no equivocation in Jeb's voice as he said, nearly the same as he had that first evening, "Good luck, Saved by the Belle."

Not *M'riah* or even *girl*.

"Goodbye, Jeb," Mariah choked out, barely making it into her car and out of sight before the tears came.

Saved by the Belle. How she rued the impulse that had goaded her into giving that name to her business, for her business was herself. It seemed the height of conceit to believe she might have a hand in turning around people's lives for the better. That she might save them—from whom? Or what?

She sniffed, swiping her nose indelicately across the back of her hand. Jeb was actually the one who'd tried to save her this afternoon, and she knew she would never forget that noble effort. How uniquely Texan he was, like the bois d'arc tree he told stories about: unapologizing for being prickly and rough on the outside, because inside lay conviction, durable and enduring as the century-old bois d'arc blocks that still supported the structures atop them as well as the day they were built.

No, he didn't need her. Not at all.

"Is Mariah stayin' for supper?" Robin asked, meeting Jeb at the door and looking fresh scrubbed and hopeful.

Placing one ankle on the opposite knee, he concentrated on tugging off his damp shoes and socks, which he left outside on the porch to dry. "No, she had to get on back to Sherman."

Robin's face fell. "Oh. Well, maybe when she comes next week, we can teach her how to rig her own rod, maybe even how to tie a good strong pallomar knot." She grinned, looking suddenly more like Wiley than either Cody or Jeb or Lisa. "And we won't let her get away so easy next time, even if we have to hog-tie her," she stated in a perfect imitation of her great-uncle's inflection.

"It's a pretty tight fit gettin' four around the table for a proper dinner," he hedged. He didn't have the heart right now to correct her assumption that Mariah would be back— or that she had even been interested in learning to fish in the first place this afternoon.

Glancing up, he found Wiley studying him through the conversation window from the kitchen. "I hear tell you pert near took all the challenge out of the experience by practically layin' a big 'un right at Mariah's feet."

"Yeah, well, that's my job, keepin' the customer satisfied," he quipped. Jeb wondered what else Robin had told Wiley—such as how it would have taken a crowbar to pry his and Mariah's gazes away from each other the whole afternoon. Even if Robin hadn't disclosed that information, he still didn't feel like letting Wiley's blue scrutiny ferret it out right now.

"I need a shower," Jeb said, not waiting for his uncle's

concurrence as he made his way down the hall to the bath-room.

Once there, he braced one palm on the edge of the sink as, avoiding his gaze, he watched his other hand scrub over his chin and wondered whether to shave or let it go another day. As if anyone would notice or care. Wasn't as if he had anybody to impress.

So. He would be unable to avoid his own thoughts, much as he wanted to.

He'd done it again. Struck the mother lode of stupidity. What was the saying? "Fool me once, shame on you; fool me twice, shame on me."

But he had thought Mariah was different. He'd thought he might have something to offer her that was missing from her life. Thought there might be some appeal in that pack-age, which he'd seen her eyeing all day long. Except ap-parently that was all it was—a temptation. In him and the redneck recreation he could provide her. Good for some thrills, but not what you'd call real marriage material.

At least she'd been honest with him. At least she'd learned *her* lesson, not to make the mistake again of falling for a man who couldn't live up to her standards. Of not mistaking physical attraction or the lure of an image for something more.

Of course, that had been the kind of bait he'd used.

Jeb peeled off the rest of his clothes and stepped into the shower, wondering what the situation had been between Mariah and her ex, Stephen.

The possibility hit him with the same force as the spray of water in his face. Not *the* Stephen Duncan? Jeb would have had to live in Outer Mongolia not to have heard of the guy whose family fairly defined old Dallas money. *That* was the man who hadn't lived up to Mariah's expectations?

What in the hell did she want from a man?

Except he had seen the pain evident in her doe brown eyes, heard it in her soft, cultured voice as she admitted she wasn't all Stephen expected her to be, either. So what had Stephen Duncan expected of Mariah that she'd felt she couldn't live with? How had *she* not measured up?

He poured a dollop of shampoo into his palm and lathered his hair, only then struck by the memory of Mariah's fingers similarly in his hair today. On the heels of that thought came one of her hands kneading his chest, her soft whimpers when he'd sought and found her pleasure points. And she'd responded fully, a single match set to kindling.

Yes, she'd been fire in his arms; he'd been seconds from sending them both up in flames.

He couldn't begin to imagine how a man might find such passion less than completely fulfilling.

Jeb gritted his teeth. But of course—that had been the bait he'd risen to.

He had to give Mariah credit for doing her job. He *had* been saved by the belle today, by being saved from one. Two, actually. Both her and Anita, for Jeb admitted to himself that he, too, like Mariah, did not believe he should be the one to change. Hadn't believed it all those years ago, when Anita had wanted him to, either. And in these past few weeks, his mistake had been in thinking he must compensate somehow to meet her standards. Hers and Mariah's.

Well, no more. He was what he was.

So now he was on his own again. He couldn't help but deem himself better off this way, even if he knew his nights would be even more restless for many weeks to come.

Five minutes later, he'd dressed and returned to the kitchen, where Wiley and Robin had already taken their places at the small corner table. He squeezed into his chair against the wall.

A short grace was said, food dished up, before anyone spoke.

Of course it was Wiley. "You know, I've been thinkin' this place is too small for us now. I've been feeling cramped as a sardine in a can. What say we go over to

Denison or Sherman this weekend and look at one of them new double-wides? Or maybe a prefab jobby? I understand some of 'em these days got four bedrooms and enough livin' area so's everyone in the family can feel like they have their own space and privacy.''

A forkful of mashed potatoes stopped halfway to Jeb's mouth. He looked at his uncle, who gazed back at him innocently. ''I wouldn't go makin' any plans to expand just yet,'' he said dourly.

Too late he realized how Robin might interpret his words—that there wasn't room for her.

''What I meant,'' he added, ''is we should take a look at our expenses first, see if something like that was even affordable.''

Out of the corner of his eye, he saw Robin set her fork and knife on the edge of her plate and put her hands in her lap, looking ever so the proper little lady, despite her surroundings and clothes. He guessed he owed Mariah that much.

''I could give up my music lessons,'' she offered. ''That'd save money and get that big piano out of here.''

He'd have teased her about making such a sacrifice except he could see she was completely serious. Reaching around the corner of the table, he gave her arm a quick squeeze. ''Now, don't worry about money, Robbie. We're doin' fine. But if you don't want to take piano anymore, then let's not do it. In fact, I've been thinkin' you might want to take some horseback-riding lessons after school instead. Didn't you say once you'd been gettin' into that horsey stuff before your mom and dad…that is, before you came to live here on Texoma?''

''Yeah.'' Robin blinked. ''What does Mariah say about it?''

''Well, now, that's something we don't have to worry about.'' He stalled, taking a bite of potatoes and chewing. ''Y'see, we had a, uh, a talk. And we agreed that while we'd made a lot of progress, it's up to me—you and me, I mean—from here on out."

He recalled Mariah wondering whether she helped or hindered them, and Jeb had taken her to mean they should cut their losses, that the effort was next door to a lost cause.

Jeb gazed at Robin, so sweet and earnest and lovable.

It couldn't be a lost cause. He vowed it wouldn't be. He may be a simple man, but he was honest, worked hard at making a living and could provide a proper home for Robin by himself.

Or was he just making excuses to give himself a reason not to change?

"I know you liked Mariah, Robbie," he said with all the confidence he could muster. "But we don't need her. We'll make it just fine."

The girl merely stared at him quizzically, eyebrows puckered, as if she were trying to make up her mind about what he meant—or simply about him. He shot a glance at Wiley, whose own scrutiny was not questioning but knowing.

Fine, he thought, loading another mound of mashed potatoes onto his fork and shoving it into his mouth. So now there were three sets of blue eyes—Robin's, Wiley's and his own—he'd have to work to avoid.

Maybe it'd keep his mind off the melting-toffee brown ones that had seemed anything but judgmental as he'd held their owner in his arms.

Chapter Eight

Through her rearview mirror, Mariah caught a brief sight of gravel rooster-tailing from the back tires of her car as she accelerated down the lane to the Albright home. She squinted against the dappling sunlight, looking for signs of trouble. Of what kind, she didn't know, only that there must be something very wrong. All she knew was Jeb had called and said he needed her, to please come right away.

She'd been helpless not to comply.

It had been two weeks since she'd seen him. Two weeks of renewed effort put into her business, two weeks of looking after her clients' every need.

Two weeks of going without looking to her own.

Mariah had parked and gotten out of her car before she saw Jeb on the dock securing his boat, apparently having just taken it out. She noticed he wore not his usual T-shirt and jeans but a green polo-style knit shirt and a pair of well-fitting twill slacks. Had he gone fishing in such attire?

But of course he wouldn't have, she realized, just as she registered that Robin was nowhere in sight.

He had been out looking for his niece—on the lake.

"Jeb!" Mariah called, already on the run, her heart in her throat. At her call, he lifted his head and started toward her in ground-eating strides, tension in every line of his body.

Mariah couldn't stop herself; she held out her hands to him, needing to give him comfort, strength, reassurance, whatever she could give him. Reaching her, he took her hands in his, his grip nearly crushing.

"She's gone, Mariah," he said roughly. "Wiley and I have looked everywhere for her. He's still out, took the pickup to search up and down the road."

"But why? What happened?"

He released her fingers and turned away, both hands shooting through his gilded brown hair. "It's my fault. I should have handled it different." His fingers linked behind his neck as he stared at the ground. "I should have handled *her* different, from the very first. And now my chances to do so have run out. The social worker from the district court'll be here any minute for the home-study interview that'll make or break my case for keepin' Robin."

"Tell me what happened," Mariah commanded gently. "I can't help until I know."

He nodded, still not looking at her. "When Robin got home from school, I told her to put on one of her new outfits and do her hair up nice so's to make a good impression. But for some reason, she chose that exact moment to stick her chin out and say somethin' about how she didn't want to look like some too-good stuffy lady, like you—I'm sorry, Mariah," he apologized quickly, his gaze cutting to her. "I shouldn't have repeated that to you."

"It doesn't matter. Just go on."

He sighed. "Anyway, I probably wasn't the most patient, but I was in kind of a rush. One of the down-riggers was jammin' on me, my grease gun was clogged, there was lube all over everything and I still had to get the blasted rigger returned to its spool before I could get myself cleaned up.

Finally I said to hell with it, I'd deal with it later. I was pretty short with Robin, tellin' her she could stick her hair up under a Dolly Parton wig for all I cared, just to get straightened up without any sass, before I headed for the shower. I'd just gotten dressed when I heard this scream from outside.''

The hand he raised to massage his forehead was shaking. ''I rushed out of the house and looked down the slope to see Robin struggling with something on the boat, like she was caught. And I knew it was the rigger. Mariah, I swear my guts turned to water. I've seen people lose fingers, getting them caught in the cable. I tore down there, but by some miracle she'd already worked herself loose, even if she did get this big red welt on her arm. I asked her what in God's name she thought she was doin', and she said she'd been thinkin' to take a look at the rigger herself. The sleeve of her brand-new blouse had gotten snagged in the cable when she pressed the Up button, and she couldn't reach the button to stop the cable from reeling in.''

Jeb stood deathly still, fighting for composure. Then he burst out, ''Damn it, she *knows* better than to fool with that equipment! I'm sure I was harder on her than I should have been, or meant to be—and you can stop lookin' at me like that right now,'' he ordered. ''I couldn't have laid a hand on that little girl if her life *had* depended on it.''

His gaze was fierce upon her, demanding her understanding. ''I was just so angry with her for bein' careless and for monkeying with something so dangerous. Mariah, all I could think of is, what if it hadn't been just her sleeve? What if she'd gotten her...gotten her hair caught in the cable?''

The mere thought of such a possibility made Mariah's own stomach turn. ''I don't blame you for being angry, Jeb,'' she assured him. ''So what did you do?''

''I gave her a good dressing-down, said something pretty stupid about how even if she may not want to put her hair up for style's sake, she sure as shootin' wasn't comin' around my boat with it flyin' every which way.''

"I see." That had been pretty stupid, but she didn't think Jeb needed to hear so right now. "And what did Robin do?''

"She—'' Closing his eyes, Jeb shook his head wearily, as if the burden he shouldered had just grown tenfold. "She just looked at me with such...disappointment in her eyes. I didn't know what to do, so I told her I thought it'd be best if we both had a private think about the situation before takin' it any further. It didn't seem quite right sending her to the boat house, like Wiley did with me and Cody, so I sent her to her room, and *I* took to the boat house, figuring I could use the time to calm down before mendin' fences with Robin and get us both set before the social worker arrived. But when I went back to the house, she'd disappeared."

Hands fisted at his sides, he stared out across the water, his gaze, as always, searching. "Help me get her back, Mariah. I'll do whatever it takes," he said hoarsely. "I just can't lose her now."

Mariah knew he meant much more than just finding Robin today. And once again she was drawn in by his willingness to do whatever it took to see to his niece's happiness.

She thrust her own fists into the pockets of her slacks to keep from reaching out to him, wanting to give him whatever *she* could offer to help him on his quest. "First of all, Jeb, you must stop beating yourself up for giving Robin the scolding she deserved. I don't fault you your reaction, even if I might not have isolated Robin at that particular moment. Knowing her, I think your own disappointment and admonishment were quite enough to impress upon her the seriousness of her transgression. Girls are different from boys in that they don't always need further emphasis of just how badly they behaved.''

"I see that now, but at the time I plain didn't know what to do. I was fit to be tied. Part of it was sheer nerves. Still is." He nodded up the lane. "That social worker'll be here any minute. What's it gonna look like, Robin running away?"

"Don't worry about that right now. Let's find Robin." Mariah concentrated, trying once again to think like an eleven-year-old girl, praying she could. What was it like to feel inadequate, that nothing you could do or be would be enough? To believe she had done all she could, and have a man tell her she hadn't it in her to fit in?

It was enough to make a woman want to wash her hands of all things male. Which would be darn difficult out here.

Mariah glanced around. "Where's Lucy?"

"Lucy?" Jeb asked distractedly. "I don't know. I haven't seen her since—" Realization struck. "You think Robin might have taken Lucy somewhere?"

"Or the dog took Robin somewhere. I've noticed Lucy wanders wherever she pleases. Do you know where she goes on her jaunts?"

"Some. I've gone looking for her up and down the lake-shore more than once and turned around, ready to give up, only to find her behind me like she'd appeared from no-where."

"Well, so we'll look for Lucy and hope to find Robin. I don't have a better idea of where to start." She eyed his still-agitated expression. "And I think it might be best if I went to search for them alone. You stay here and prepare yourself for when the social worker arrives."

"She won't come out of hiding if she doesn't want to. Lucy, that is—though it seems like Robin, too," Jeb said ruefully.

"Then we need to give her an incentive. Do you have some sort of dog treat that Lucy finds irresistible?"

He looked at her askance for a moment, then nodded

rather grimly. "If there's one thing I do know, it's what kind of bait to put on a hook."

Fifteen minutes later, after whistling and waving around a gingerly held, rather greasy barbecued pig ear—a *real* one—which Jeb had assured her was sheer ambrosia to a dog, Mariah found Lucy. Willingly she relinquished the redolent treat to the dog as she scanned the area. She had a feeling Robin was close by.

Sure enough, she found the girl sitting far back under an outcropping of limestone, her long legs tucked up to her chin. There was mud on both knees of her pants, and her hair had twigs and leaves tangled in it. Mariah's heart twisted when she saw the rent in Robin's sleeve and the ugly red welt on her forearm.

The girl eyed Mariah distrustfully, and Mariah remembered Jeb saying how Robin had wanted nothing to do with looking like a too-good, stuffy lady. Likely Robin had a bone to pick with her, too, for terminating their relationship without a goodbye or an explanation, and Mariah realized how remiss she herself had been in seeing to Robin's needs. But such explanations and apologies could wait.

"Your uncle's worried half to death about you," Mariah said quietly.

Robin said nothing, merely set her chin obstinately and switched her gaze to stare out across the lake.

Mariah clasped her hands behind her back. "You know, Jeb Albright may not be quite the natural at grasping the intricate workings of the female mind as he is at fishing, but his greatest concern in life is for the happiness of those he loves. And that's nothing a girl should turn her nose up at, if you ask me."

That said, she turned, calling Lucy to her side as she picked her way over the uneven ground along the lakeshore, heading back to the Albrights'.

She'd gone no more than fifty feet when Robin caught

up with her, her expression no longer sullen so much as bemused. They had walked side by side another hundred feet before she burst out, "Why'd you stop workin' with Uncle Jeb?"

Mariah paid extra attention to her footing among the white, black and slate gray rocks. "What did your uncle tell you about that?"

"He said it was up to us from here on out. That we didn't need you anymore."

"You don't," Mariah freely admitted. "I'm sorry, Robin, for not telling you myself. Truly I thought I was doing what was best for you."

"The best for *me*, huh?" There was another period of silence. Then, somewhat impertinently, Robin asked, "So why is it nothin's been the same for Uncle Jeb since you stopped coming?" Blue eyes, so like her uncle's, flashed up at Mariah. "And nothin' *I* do seems to make things better!"

As if angry with herself for making such an admission, the girl literally flung herself away from Mariah, nearly falling as she tripped over the stony ground. Ten paces away, she turned back toward Mariah.

"He's not just a redneck fishing guide, y'know!" she shouted before spinning around again and bolting up the beach.

Mariah stared after her, her thoughts whirling.

A cold nose poked itself into her palm as her hand hung at her side. Mariah glanced down. Lucy sat at her feet, head and shoulders swaying from the force of her wagging tail. She gazed up at Mariah hopefully.

"No more sow ears," she apologized, holding out her hands for Lucy to sniff. Then she lifted her chin and located Robin again. Or perhaps, she should say, no more sow's ear—or trying to make a silk purse from one in no need of changing.

* * *

Jeb was chatting, albeit distractedly, with the social worker, Cathy Sperry, when he heard a voice coming from the direction of the dock. He turned just in time to see Robin marching up the slope, Mariah trailing behind.

The girl stopped in her tracks at the sight of him. For an enduring moment, they just gazed at each other uncertainly, and Jeb knew Robin was waiting to take her lead from him as he stood with her *guardian ad litem* at his side. He hesitated, wondering desperately how to play this scene out. Then he noticed the way she held her torn sleeve closed, her other arm braced protectively over it, and the terrifying scene of a few hours earlier was painted vividly before his eyes.

Uncrossing his own arms, Jeb took a step toward the girl.

It was all the encouragement Robin needed. Hair streaming out behind her, she raced up the incline and threw her arms around his middle, clinging to him like a vine. And Jeb held her as closely, bending over her, pressing his large hand to her dark blond head and rocking her as if she were a child half as old.

"I'm s-sorry, Uncle Jeb," she sobbed, face pressed against his shirtfront. "I w-was tryin' to help you, n-not be a bother. I remembered you s-said how my dad was good at tinkering with things, and I thought I might could fix the rigger. I didn't mean to get my sleeve caught—"

"I know, Robbie," he murmured, his arm around her shoulders tightening reflexively. "Don't cry. It's all right, I promise."

But she wasn't to be so easily consoled as a mere pup of a child. As if a dam had burst inside her, Robin surged on in a torrent of words. "It's 'cause I'm a girl! All I do is c-cost you money and trouble, with all the c-clothes and lessons and that stupid slumber party."

Jeb frowned. "I thought you enjoyed havin' your friends over." He brushed her hair away from her face. "And you seemed to like the pretty clothes, at least at first, just as you liked doin' your hair up.''

"I know I did," she cried, as if confessing to a terrible crime, "but I don't want to be different from you and Wiley! Because you...you won't want me anymore if I don't fit in!''

Robin broke down in a fresh bout of weeping as, completely bewildered, Jeb looked to Mariah. She only shook her head, apparently equally puzzled. He was on his own here.

He crouched in front of the girl, gripping her upper arms as he stared up at her. "Robin, where would you ever get an idea like that?''

"F-from you! First you said you were hiring Mariah to help you learn to be a better parent to a girl, then you said we didn't need her, and I thought it was 'cause you'd decided learning how to deal with girls was more trouble than it was worth. Because I could tell you liked her and she liked you, so why else would you want to stop seeing her?''

"I...well, that's between Mariah and me. But I will tell you we both were putting your welfare first."

"See, that's what I mean! You weren't happy when she wasn't comin' around anymore, and I knew it was because of me and I didn't know what to do to make things better. You kept talking about horseback-riding lessons and encouragin' me goin' to play after school with my friends, like you didn't want my help anymore. And I thought if I did stop helping altogether at the store or with your fishing business, you wouldn't need me at all, and it wouldn't matter so much to you if I had to go live with Aunt Anita."

Jeb shot a quick look at the social worker, who was taking the whole scene in with great interest. At the moment, he couldn't find it in him to care all that much what sort of impression he was making. He needed to get to the bottom of this matter with his niece.

"Robin...Robbie, that's not how it was at all. I'd only

been tryin' to spare you worry, but I think I better tell you now that, even though Mariah's and my goal *was* to teach me how to better meet your needs as you grow into a young woman, what I really was hoping to do was boost my chances of keeping custody of you.''

Robin sniffed. "You were?"

"Y'see, I knew I was at a disadvantage, bein' a bachelor livin' out here with my own uncle without much to offer a girl by way of feminine advice or support. I'm not even a real parent, much less a female one who would know instinctively how you were feelin' and what you were goin' through. Heck, I didn't even have a mother growing up I could take my cues from.''

"But that's why you *do* know what I'm goin' through," Robin protested, crying harder. "Isn't that why you told me that story about Dad?" Evidently mindful, too, of who listened, she went on with a fierce loyalty, "You understand me better than anyone else ever, ever could, don't you think so?"

And despite who listened, Jeb knew he couldn't lie. "I think...I think this whole incident pretty much proves I haven't.''

Still grasping Robin's arms, he dropped his chin to his chest for a long moment, then raised it to return his gaze to his niece's tear-streaked face. "I know you haven't had the contact with your aunt Anita you've had with me and Wiley, but I believe she's as devoted as we are to seeing to your best interests.''

That had been said to let Ms. Sperry know he wouldn't do anything so disreputable as bad-mouth the contending party in this case, as if this were a nasty divorce. The next statement, though, he made for Robin's benefit, to get her thinking of a possibility he himself hadn't yet had the fortitude to dwell on. "If you did have to...get to go live with Anita, she'd take good care of you and treat you like you were her own daughter.''

Robin's mouth trembled. "But she's got a family already."

"That's what would be so nice for you." He tried to put the conviction lacking in his voice into his eyes. "Sure, there'd be adjustments for everyone, but you'd need to give it a chance—"

"I don't understand!" Fresh tears spilled down her cheeks. "You and Dad s-stayed here with Uncle Wiley—"

"Your dad and I didn't have a choice. I'm not saying I'd have chosen any differently. Wiley did the best he could by us and made a darn fine job of it, if I do say so myself." He shook her gently in emphasis. "But *you*... you do have a choice, Robin, and I *wouldn't* be doing my best by you if I didn't consider that alternative."

She shook her head mutely, her thin face awash with tears and misery. "Don't you want me to stay with you, Uncle Jeb?" she whispered brokenly. "D-don't you think I can ever belong here, even if I am a girl?"

Jeb swallowed back the lump that sprang into his throat. Her question was so similar to the one that had driven him at the age of six as he struggled to find a foothold in the shifting sands of his drastically changed existence: would he ever be enough?

And Robin's best interests or not, nothing on earth could have stopped him from responding to her cry for understanding.

"Oh, Robbie. Of course I do," he said, his voice cracking. "I'd want you to stay with me even if you were as much trouble as a hornet's nest. And even if you couldn't rig a line or fix a down-rigger for love or money, even if you went away and lived somewhere else for twenty years, you'd always belong right here on Texoma."

With a choked sob of relief, Robin again flung herself into his arms, burying her face against his neck as he did in hers, self-reproach at his obliviousness to Robin's real needs eating its way through his very vitals.

Wiley showed up at that moment, almost as many questions in his eyes as were in those of Cathy Sperry. Jeb deemed it best to try to salvage as soon as possible what he could from this disastrous afternoon.

Giving his niece a final squeeze, he rose. "Wiley, I'd appreciate your takin' Robin inside and treating that welt on her arm, give her a hand washin' up and help her in picking out some clean clothes." Mariah was probably the more logical choice for such a task, but they had to learn to get along without her. "I'd like to have a word with Ms. Sperry, decide whether to go on with the interview today or make it for another afternoon."

"Will do," Wiley replied, setting a grizzled hand on the girl's crown and giving her already tousled hair a fond rumple, as one would normally do to a boy rather than a girl. Still, Jeb saw Robin's expression reveal more relief. All she wanted from either of her uncles was what they had in them to give.

Sticking that thought into a corner of his mind for later reflection, Jeb turned back to the social worker. And Mariah.

She seemed to sense his next words and forestalled them by saying, "I'd like to stay, Jeb, if I may. Perhaps I can help you explain just exactly what our arrangement was."

He saw the familiar caring concern in her eyes, and God help him, Jeb didn't have the will right now to refuse her support. The fact of the matter was, Ms. Sperry had seen one terribly upset little girl with a nasty-looking scrape on her arm, and he'd already pegged the midthirtyish woman as knowing her job.

It didn't look good for him.

Well, there was nothing left to do but get the whole story out and make an assessment of what his chances were.

"So, Mr. Albright, let me see if I understand the situation correctly," Cathy Sperry said after he was through telling her the series of events leading up to today, helped along by Mariah's clarifying interjections. "You hired Ms. Duncan, a professional organizer with no children of her own, to help you learn how to better raise your niece."

"Yes." He ordered himself not to turn red. Put baldly like that, his plan did seem a little half-baked.

"I've nothing against Ms. Duncan here, you understand, but why was it you considered her—with a background primarily in society-event planning—particularly suited to assist you in your goal?" Ms. Sperry gestured, raising one hand, palm up. "I mean, I'd think you'd look to one of the mothers of your niece's friends for advice, or one of her teachers."

"Well, I can see your point," Jeb replied, willing away his awkwardness at answering such a question, not daring to look directly at Mariah. "But I was sort of in a bind, what with the hearing comin' up fast. I needed to get some good, solid input."

This wasn't looking any better. But how could he explain the sheer panic he'd felt at the thought of losing Robin to Anita? How totally inadequate he'd felt measured against the kind of home life she could offer Robin?

But he'd also wanted to prove to Anita he was not a backwater hick lacking the depth or understanding or resources to see to Robin's particular needs—or the particular needs of a woman. And in that aim, Jeb realized, he hadn't been entirely upstanding. In fact, the incident with Robin today had happened because of that not quite aboveboard intention. Because he had tried to play Anita's game on her level. He'd been bound to fail from the very start.

He knew he must avoid compounding the mistake however he could, even if he wasn't ready to admit, at least not altogether, to wanting to one-up Anita Babcock. "What I mean is, I chose Mariah to help me with Robin because I could tell she was a real…a real lady."

From the corner of his vision, he saw Mariah stiffen imperceptibly at his assertion, as if offended. He'd seen such a reaction before from her and had always been puzzled by it. But he'd only told the truth. She *was* a real lady, deserving of every bit of a man's respect and devotion.

"And just why was it you decided to discontinue the association between you and Ms. Duncan?"

Yes, honesty must be his course right now. "While we both believed we—I—had made some progress, we decided Robin and I would be better off just going along as I had been, doing the best I could for her."

Jeb lifted one shoulder in acknowledgment and acceptance. "I am what I am, and that wasn't going to change all that much in the space of a few weeks. If I *was* going to do my best for Robin, I needed to learn to relate to her in my own way."

She appeared to digest this, nodding reflectively before turning to Mariah. "And your opinion, Ms. Duncan?"

"I completely agreed with that assessment of the situation." Elbow braced on her forearm, Mariah hooked two fingers under the strand of pearls at her neck in that familiar gesture of security. "I simply didn't believe Jeb or Robin needed my...my services. Despite the strikes against him and how he tried to diminish them, his intention from the beginning had always been to see to his niece's happiness."

He was gladdened by her understanding, but Jeb wondered what Mariah would really think of him if she found out he hadn't acted quite so honorably in this whole matter.

"And yet, Mr. Albright, you turned to Ms. Duncan for help today in handling your niece," Ms. Sperry countered.

Oh, yes, Cathy Sperry knew her job. The woman didn't miss much. "I did, and I won't apologize for calling her," he answered frankly. "I had to find Robin, and I would have done whatever I needed to ensure her safe return, even if it meant admitting I couldn't get that done on my own."

Adjusting her eyeglasses, the social worker pursed her lips for a few moments before again turning her astute scrutiny on Mariah. "So, Ms. Duncan, *are* you going to be a continuing influence in both Mr. Albright's and his niece's lives?''

Mariah's lashes fell—apparently she felt as he did that she must guard her gaze—and some of the shine was taken off of Jeb's consolation at her earlier endorsement when she murmured softly, ''No. That was never the plan.''

''I see.'' Musingly the other woman tapped her fingernail against one front tooth for another interminable moment.

Jeb couldn't stand it; he had to ask. ''So how's it look, Ms. Sperry? I mean, for Robin staying here with me?''

She took a deep breath and let it out with a shake of her head. ''I can make no judgment either way until I've heard all the facts from both parties, especially when I'm still not completely clear on just how Robin's distress today was brought on by this whole situation with Ms. Duncan and whatever her purpose has been here.''

''It's not Mariah's fault, or Robin's, if this plan went awry,'' Jeb asserted. ''I take full responsibility. And I know on the surface it probably seems a little ill conceived, but it *was* well-intentioned. I love Robin and want only the best for her.''

''Yes, that at least does seem to be obvious.'' Ms. Sperry chewed on her lower lip. ''Let's talk for a moment about your other plans, Mr. Albright. Do you have any, to marry and raise a family, that is?''

''You mean, like—'' Caught off-guard, Jeb stammered. ''Like, in the works?''

''I mean, specifically, do you want that sort life, with a wife and children? Or are you content with your existence as it is now?'' For the first time, she smiled. ''Please believe me, I'm not criticizing your life-style choice in the slightest. I'm merely concerned whether being a husband and a father is part of what you feel you need to be happy and would pursue of your own accord, even without having one of the roles thrust upon you.''

''I guess I never thought about it,'' he equivocated, shamelessly breaking his recent vow to be honest. Because he had thought about the matter. Had dreamed of it—with Mariah. Perhaps foolishly, most likely unwisely. And he just wasn't up to admitting to even a part of that fantasy right now, even if he was afraid the eagle-eyed Cathy Sperry would see past the smoke and mirrors and figure it out for herself.

As long as Mariah didn't figure it out, that was all that mattered. Yes, he'd needed her today, and she had come with her normal willingness to help however she could, but the situation remained the same: Mariah Duncan might be mightily attracted to him, but consider him real marriage material she did not.

Behind her glasses, Ms. Sperry's gaze was keen upon him. "Perhaps it would be best if I gave you some time to think over a few of these questions," the social worker suggested. "And to give you and Robin a chance to re-group. Regardless of how tough I might be on you, Mr. Albright, I want as much as you do for you to make the best impression, and I'll give you every opportunity to do that."

Now Jeb studied Cathy Sperry. He wondered if she'd already interviewed the Babcocks and what conclusions she'd made from that visit. Wondered if she'd already discerned the years-old forces at work beneath the surface, pushing and pulling at each other without any real sense of what the ultimate consideration should be: a little girl's happiness.

And that must be his biggest priority.

She dipped into her purse to pull out her calendar. "Shall we reschedule our interview for next Thursday, same time?"

Jeb nodded, both as a reminder to himself and assent. "Next Thursday will be fine, Ms. Sperry. I look forward to talking to you at length."

And from here on out, he wouldn't make the mistake of trying to be something he was not.

Chapter Nine

After the social worker left, Jeb stood unmoving in the gathering dusk, discouragement evident in every line of his body. Mariah ached to comfort him, to offer support and reassurance, but no convincing words came to mind. The situation certainly did not look encouraging.

He glanced toward the trailer, and she guessed he was trying to decide how he would explain it to Robin and Wiley.

"Let's take a walk," she suggested, much as he had the first evening she'd come out here. "They'll survive a while longer without you."

Nodding, he fell into step beside her as she chose the course, taking him, for lack of a better option, to the secluded spot where she'd discovered Lucy and Robin. "Just so you know next time," she explained, "should one of them disappear."

Stooping, Jeb pushed aside a branch and peered into the cubbyhole where Robin had taken refuge. After a moment he straightened, still squinting into the shadows that grew deeper by the minute as he broke a twig from the branch. "Yeah. Maybe I'll know better next time."

From behind him, Mariah sent a hand out toward him as he stripped the twig of its leaves, shaking his head slowly. "God, what a bunch of misfits we must've seemed today, us two hayseed bachelors trying to console a hysterical little girl who's wonderin' why she can't just be one of the guys. Oh, and with our etiquette coach standing by like an emergency backup. Even *I* wouldn't give me custody of Robin after that ridiculous scene."

He cut a quick glance at her, then dropped his chin to concentrate on halving the twig, then again, before tossing the pieces away with an impatient sound. "I can't believe I didn't see what she'd been goin' through."

"Jeb, you weren't—"

"No, there's no excuse! I should have *known* what was wrong with her, what she was feeling." The self-recriminations poured out of him, and Mariah decided for now just to let him get it out of his system, much as he had let Robin do this afternoon. "I mean, my own parents' deaths may have happened twenty-five years ago, but I do understand what it's like to have that terrible insecurity inside of not being enough and wonderin' if I'd find a place I belonged again. And *still* I was blind to it, had no idea what my plans and schemes were doing to her," he finished with complete disgust.

"What 'schemes'?" Mariah asked. "You wanted to learn how to be the best parent you could to Robin. You've done nothing but put her needs and desires first, from the very beginning."

"Have I?" He pointed in the direction of their property, his eyes managing to look intensely blue even in the dwindling light. "Then you tell me, why did that happen today? God—" he spun away from her, fists plunging into the pockets of his trousers "—I probably just blew every chance in the world I had for keeping Robin! When it comes right down to it, maybe she doesn't belong here, surrounded by all these hazards, both natural and man-made. And if not here, then…''

He stooped and picked up a stone, brushing his thumb back and forth across its surface. But he didn't skip it across the water as Mariah thought he would; he turned without warning and threw it, hard, so hard she didn't hear the splash. "Damn it, Anita's gotten everything she wanted out of life! A well-to-do husband, two kids, probably a white picket fence with a cat and dog in the yard!"

He dragged his hand through his hair as he said more quietly yet somehow much more vehemently, "So *why* can't I have…what I want most?"

The raw emotion in that question tore at her, so like her own frustration and feelings of inadequacy. Unable to prevent herself from doing so, Mariah laid her hand on Jeb's forearm in what she knew was meager consolation, as were her words. "I know you didn't answer Cathy Sperry when she asked, but surely you wouldn't always be without a wife who could be a mother to Robin? You're likely to marry one day, aren't you?"

He stared at her hand where it lay on his arm, and she remembered when she'd made a like gesture of comfort—and the results: Jeb kissing her, almost in challenge. This time he wrenched his gaze away to stare out across the lake, where a string of lights twinkled.

"It's not what I'd call a sure thing," he said tersely.

"You said, though, that the only sure thing in life is that we'll learn nothing if we don't remain open to all sorts of possibilities, continue to believe the best about people, about life, about…ourselves." His statement had resonated in the deepest depths of Mariah's heart, becoming part of her own dilemma, part of its solution. "And—"

That laser-direct gaze came back around to hers. Yes, his eyes were like windows where the curtains had been thrown back, the blinds raised, making what he saw just as clear as what was seen. "And?" he echoed.

"And..." Miserably Mariah dropped her chin, unable to maintain eye contact. She wanted so much to help this man, truly help him as she felt she still had yet to do. But she was fighting, as she had from the beginning, her own feelings that she had nothing definite or tangible to offer Jeb and his niece. And much as he blamed himself for today's incident, Mariah knew she owned part of it, too, for she hadn't made their lives any better, as she'd claimed Saved by the Belle always did.

And Jeb knew that. Knew she, too, had failed—failed him and Robin. The knowledge sliced through her heart. She could deny it no longer—there really wasn't a place for her Southern values in the real world. Or at least not in Jeb's world...

Suddenly Mariah knew, with her woman's intuition or whatever, the real reason Jeb had hired her in particular to help him with Robin, what he felt he had to come up with in order to compete with the home life Anita Babcock would provide Robin.

What he felt would be used against him.

And the way to help Jeb came to her in a flash of comprehension.

"What if...no." She shook her head. How could she presume—again—to know how to "fix" things for him?

"What?" he pressed. "Mariah, I'm willing to try practically anything."

Yes, he was; he always had been. Encouraged, she blurted out, "Well, what if *we* got married?"

"If we got *what*?" Jeb asked incredulously, not exactly the reaction she might have hoped for—and much like his reaction the first time she'd mentioned Saved by the Belle.

Mariah hesitated again, wondering if she was being incredibly naive. She'd been so before, believing Stephen's story about the reason for his infidelity being her inability to understand a man's basic needs, and letting that criticism rule most every action of hers since. She *must* be wiser, more cautious, more realistic—

Oh, but she must remain hopeful, too, mustn't she?

"It'd do the trick, wouldn't it?" Mariah forged on. "You'd not only show the court that Robin would have a father *and* a mother, just like with the Babcocks, but you'd also demonstrate that she would always have someone to provide a proper feminine influence on her. I mean, I am a real Southern belle, aren't I? Look what I named my business."

Jeb simply stared at her, not entirely resembling the stunned and disbelieving striper he'd hauled out of the lake for her a few weeks ago. But close.

"Oh, stop looking at me like that!" she demanded, her tone made short by her embarrassment. Lord, she was making a fool of herself. She lifted her chin. "It's not such a ridiculous suggestion, you know! It'd take care of everyone's problems."

"Your 'problems' included?" he asked ever so softly.

Virtually clutching the pearls at her throat, Mariah turned in another avoidance of his too-sharp gaze. Yes, she had her own needs, too, that had grown far beyond her initial goal to prove to her ex-husband that she could be appreciated for the genteel qualities she'd been raised with. But what she needed most of all still seemed impossible, mutually exclusive: a man to love her for who she was, and not because she was—or wasn't—a certain kind of woman. And because he loved her, he would need her and no one else to fulfill his desire.

"Just forget I said anything," she muttered wearily. "It *was* a ridiculous, half-baked idea."

"Oh, no," Jeb contradicted. "Let's explore your...offer. So you think we should take the plunge and get married? You'll be my barefoot fishwife, and I'll be your redneck lover."

"Don't!" she cried, spinning around to stare him in the eye. "You're *not* just a typical redneck good ol' boy, Jeb Albright, whatever that sort of man might be. Time and again I've seen you put others' concerns and needs above your own. Robin's—even mine. Why, you jumped into the lake to try and rescue me when you thought I might need it."

"And I warned you then not to go paintin' me in such a noble light," Jeb reminded her. His eyes were like two blue flames under glass. "I wonder if you have any genuine idea what you're offering...or what you'd be getting."

He bent, and before she knew what was happening, Jeb had swung her into his arms in one effortless movement. Mariah yelped, one arm clamping reflexively around his neck. The precaution was completely unnecessary. There was no danger of him dropping her even as, in three strides, he immersed them chest deep in the chilly water of Lake Texoma.

Mariah gasped, surprise and shock and fear rolling over her at once. Taking a dip in the lake during daylight was one thing; doing so after dark, when any number of unseen beasties might slither or slide or buzz around her, was quite another.

"What are you doing?" she asked, her voice shrill in her ears.

He loosened his grasp around her shoulders and under her knees to let her slide slowly down his front. Still, though, he held her against him.

"What'm I doin'?" he echoed her question in that sensuous backwoods twang. "I'm showin' you what it would mean to be married to me. No pig in a poke for you this time, girl."

Now that initial shock had worn off, she found the water strangely exhilarating as it ebbed and flowed around her, causing her chest to lap gently up against Jeb's. "W-what do you mean?"

"I mean if you're gonna go native, at least do it with your eyes wide open." One eyebrow quirked. "I won't be accused of seeming something I'm not and have you get all disappointed on me. You need to know exactly what you're getting. Exactly."

She shivered at the dangerous glint in his eye, the portent of his words. "I have no idea what you're talking about," she declared shakily.

"Then allow me to show you."

He raised one hand to touch callused fingertips to her temple, and Mariah found herself spellbound, as always, by his touch.

"It's kinda like fishing, don't you know?" he murmured whisper soft. His caress traced the line of her jaw to her chin, then down, dipping into the indentation at the base of her throat as he slid a finger under the strand of pearls nestled there.

He hesitated briefly, as if considering the worth of each perfectly formed bead. Then he laid the strand ever so gently back in its place and went on, "Y'see, I know this lake's every secret place—how deep, how wide, how fertile each recess, hollow and niche under its smooth, unruffled surface."

Lower he went, his touch made all the more intimate by the wetness of her blouse plastered against her skin as he trailed his fingertips through the valley between her breasts.

She was captured, daring not breathe, as he continued, "And I know every way imaginable to plumb those depths and make them yield to me their treasure. So you tell me—is all that, all I am, your idea of real marriage material?"

His hands drifted lower still, bumping the back of his knuckles over her ribs to her waist, then sweeping up again, the curve between forefinger and thumb shaping the underswell of her breasts.

Mariah moaned softly as she surged against him in silent invitation. Yes, she thought. He was real, as she'd sensed from the beginning. Yes, he was made of the stuff that endured and lasted a lifetime. And this was what she needed, more than life. He knew that, knew how to meet her need. How could anything else matter?

He didn't kiss her, just stared deep into her eyes as if to discover *her* every secret. The moonlight picked up the gold in his ever unruly hair and turned it silver. That effect, along with his eyes, framed by those startlingly dark, long eyelashes, made him look like no man of this earth, but the wildest of angels. An angel with a mission.

And Mariah knew she must touch the heaven in his eyes. "Kiss me, Jeb," she begged. *"Please."*

Somehow she knew that appeal was not what he wanted to hear. Still, he didn't hesitate, only muttered a short oath beneath his breath as the fingers that had been so gentle tightened around her waist and he dragged her against him, his mouth covering hers hungrily, roughly, needily. And for an instant, Mariah thought she heard the sound of beating wings.

But it wasn't anything so ethereal; it was her heart pounding in her ears. Neither was he intangible. He was all warm-blooded male, his sexuality—and identity—of an earthier kind of divinity.

For he *was* on a mission, meant to show her *exactly* what it would mean to be married to this unassuming rural man.

Mariah didn't hold back. Couldn't. She sank her fingers into his thick hair and gave herself up to the same primitive need. There was no finesse in either of them as teeth bumped against and bruised lips, roughened skin rasped over tender skin. Noses collided as mouths slanted at different angles, seeking more complete contact. Her footing floated out from beneath her, and Jeb secured her to him with the boost of both palms on her behind. She wrapped her legs around his waist as the fire between them leapt higher, the heat of their bodies warming the water around them.

Jeb tore his mouth from hers, that penetrating gaze delving into the depths of hers, mining the deepest secrets of her soul.

"Tell me what you want, Mariah," he insisted hoarsely.

"I want *you,*" she stated without equivocation, fingers clenching in his hair. "I do, Jeb."

"And?"

Mariah groaned. Oh, always that contingent "and" with him, which made her babble on when she should just leave what she'd said stand! Should she tell him all, of how she had come to love him in just a few short weeks? What if he didn't say the same? Sure, she knew now that she could kindle within him a burning desire for her. But did he love her? The question that still plagued her was: could he love her for who she was?

Her breath caught in her throat. Or perhaps it was the words. *Be wise,* he'd cautioned his niece, looking, as always, to her best interests. *Be wiser than I was.*

No, she couldn't speak, but a telling tear spilled over and ran down her cheek.

"Ah no, M'riah, don't cry," Jeb said raggedly, offering her the same comfort he'd given Robin. "It's all right, I promise." And in the next instant, they were clinging to and comforting each other, trembling with fear for what they both stood to lose, and what they suspected had already had been lost to them through no fault of their own. A certain naiveté about the world, a trustfulness about life and people.

Yet it was most definitely no longer a part of them.

Jeb sank his face into the crook of her neck, his arms holding her so close, so very close, as if he would never let her go. And she held him, too, comforted him the way she knew how.

"It *could* work, Jeb." She tugged his chin up, fingers still hopelessly tangled in the hair at his temples. "For...for Robin's sake. Think how much better chance you'd have of keeping her, and I know you want that more than anything."

For the moment, he said nothing, his respiration sharp and deep. He brought one hand up to graze the pad of his thumb across the chafed skin of her cheek.

"No," he said. "No, I don't think so. Not even for Robin."

God, it hurt to hear his refusal! But Mariah took the blow without a flinch, because he was right. Robin needed real parents, not a contrived situation, which was what she had run away from this afternoon.

Hands about her waist, he let her down slowly as shame and embarrassment swept over her, since Mariah realized that once again her motive hadn't been so noble as putting his niece's concerns first—and Jeb knew it. Knew it about both of them, and with the voice of reason called them back to sanity. To reality.

"Look what I've done," he said, voice subdued. "You're soaked to the skin, and your clothes are ruined. I'm sorry, Mariah."

"I...I'm sorry, too," Mariah stammered. Sorry for both of them. For all of them. In the real world, problems weren't so cut-and-dried that taking one particular action might magically solve them. Jeb had been the one who suggested that, way back when Wiley had called her out there that first time.

They walked in silence back to the boat house, where Jeb located towels for them to dry off with. He again offered her clean clothes, but she refused. She wanted nothing more now than to end this disastrous afternoon once and for all.

Except that would mean bringing an end, this time quite emphatically, to her association with Jeb Albright.

As always, he walked her to her car, helped her arrange a dry towel over the seat to prevent water from soaking through to the upholstery. She slid onto the seat, her heart aching that it would end this way.

Mariah looked up at him as he leaned the heels of his hands on the open window. "Well. Good luck at the hearing, Jeb."

"Thanks."

"You'll let me know how it comes out, won't you?"

He hesitated, then nodded. "Sure."

Her throat tightened as she considered what that outcome might be. "You know I care very much for both yours and Robin's happiness, don't you?" she whispered.

She saw his eyes close briefly, as if in sudden pain. Then he opened them and said, "I need to thank you, too, for comin' to *my* rescue today. Tryin' to twice, in fact, with your proposal. You don't know what it means to me that you'd be willing to do that for Robin. But I couldn't let either of us make such a rash decision."

His mouth tipped at the corner in one of his wry, solo-dimpled smiles. Except it looked sad. Sadder and wiser. "I guess you can rest easy now about there bein' truth in your advertising, since I *was* saved by the belle."

She felt she'd done much more damage than good. "You would have found Robin eventually, or she'd have come home. You *are* a good parent to her, Jeb. Don't ever believe different," Mariah urged rather desperately.

He merely shrugged, that same gesture of acceptance she'd seen him give the social worker, and it wrung her heart.

She'd never thought him more noble, had never loved him more. She simply couldn't let it end like this, rash or not.

"Jeb, I know my suggestion we get married was… extreme, but could there be a way, after the hearing, I mean, that you and I might…"

Her voice trailed off as, for the first time since she'd known him, his straight-shooting gaze avoided hers.

"There's always that possibility, I guess," he admitted, though his tone was not what she'd call hopeful.

He paused again, his features drawn, as if some emotion inside him stretched to the limit. "The fact of the matter, though," he said roughly, "is that we still come from different worlds, with whole different experiences that make us who we are. You said so yourself."

"Yes, but look how we've come to...come to respect each other for those differences. And doesn't it seem likely we could build upon that—"

"Mariah." His tone was firm. "It's best right now, I think, you give yourself some time—time to get completely over your ex. I need time, too, to get my head on straight and get back to what my priorities should be. I've let myself be distracted from them."

He made a slow perusal of his surroundings: the boat house and dock with his high-tech boat bobbing in the water next to them; the native Texas trees growing along the property line leading up to the road—catalpa, pecan, hackberry, cottonwood and the bois d'arc he'd spoken of; Bubba J.'s, now dark; the trailer, itself lit up, warmth shining from its windows.

"At least I know now how I've got to handle the situation," he said quietly as he shoved off from the car and stood tall. "How I should have handled it from the very first."

Mariah noticed there was no hint of hopefulness or optimism in his voice or manner, and she guessed that was the real progress they'd both made. So why, she asked herself as she drove away, did she feel as if she had nothing to look forward to for the rest of her days?

At the top of the hill, she stopped the car and unceremoniously tossed her organizer into the Dempsey Dumpster in front of Bubba J.'s.

* * *

Jeb heard the screen door open and close behind him as he stood on the porch and stared up at the starry sky.

"Can't sleep again tonight, son?" Wiley asked.

"Nope," he answered without turning.

"You're gonna wear yourself down to a frazzle and make yourself sick, y'know, and then what good'll you be to Robin? Or anyone else, for that matter."

A month ago he'd have taken Wiley to task for the innuendo. Now, though, Jeb let it slide right off his back.

"Well, it'll all be over, one way or the other, day after tomorrow," he said. "I'll sleep then."

"You thinkin' about how that social worker's report turned out?" Wiley asked, coming to stand beside him, the fingers of both hands tucked under opposite armpits, eyes lifting to give the sky an inspection of his own.

Jeb nodded. They'd received a copy of Cathy Sperry's report a week ago, as was the procedure. Anita would have received one, too. His lawyer had prepared him for the possibility of the adoption being decided one way or the other from that report, since a recommendation was almost always made for one party or the other, which most judges would be inclined to rubber-stamp. At that point, his lawyer had said, the situation usually resolved itself without going any further; depending upon how strongly one petitioner had been recommended in the social worker's report, the other normally deemed it judicious to withdraw his or her application for adoption rather than stretch out the inevitable with a costly court appearance and also avoid the probable turmoil such an ordeal would be for the child.

But Cathy Sperry, in an unusual turn of events, hadn't made a recommendation. Either petitioner, she'd said, would provide a healthy, loving environment for Robin.

Jeb dragged a hand through his hair. "I guess you'd say her report comes under the category of good news/bad news, the good bein' we're still in the running. The bad, I figure, bein' now the case'll definitely have to be argued in open court, where I got a feeling it could get nasty. I mean, I intend to be civil, but I'm gonna stand up for myself and who I am if I'm put under attack, as I'm guessin' will be the thrust of Anita's case.''

"Then so be it," Wiley agreed, and Jeb shot him a grateful look, glad for his uncle's support. He'd finally told Wiley what had happened between him and Anita those years ago. Not that the older man hadn't already gathered the gist of the situation, as Jeb had always suspected. It helped, though, to get it off his chest.

"Yeah," Jeb said on a sigh. "I just don't think Robin needs the distress of witnessing a confrontation between her aunt and uncle. Still, there's likely no getting around it, since I also got an idea Anita wouldn't have withdrawn her petition had the report gone in my favor, just as I sure wouldn't have given up without taking my best shot at keepin' Robin.'' Judicious or not.

Was he taking such a stand for Robin's sake? "Because," he went on quietly, "it's inevitable Anita and I would face off at some time."

At least, Jeb mused, Ms. Sperry hadn't related Robin's near-miss with the down-rigger in her report, which would have done the worst damage to him. He didn't need a legal eagle to tell him Anita's attorney would have had a field day with such ammunition. But for some reason, the social worker didn't mention the incident, even if she did recount his hiring of Mariah to help him be a better parent to a growing girl, which still was only part of the whole story. But as he had told Mariah, he had only one course to take: to be as honest as possible from here on out and leave off with the games, played mostly with himself, that had distracted him from seeing to Robin's well-being.

And the truth was he'd fallen in love with Mariah Duncan. Whether he had wanted to or not, he'd taken the bait—hook, line and sinker. Yet he couldn't be sorry for loving her. She'd taught him a few things about women—both growing and already grown—and about himself that he needed to get settled in his mind once and for all; he even had a notion he'd been able to do the same for her. The regret came in how he'd let fantasies of a future relationship with her distract him from seeing to Robin's best interests, just as his past relationship with Anita had led him to hiring Mariah in the first place. He had let her years-old rejection of him cloud his judgment, and it had nearly caused Robin terrible harm.

At the thought, his jaw clenched involuntarily. He still wasn't sure of the wisdom in telling Ms. Sperry that he and Anita had once been involved by way of explaining his rationale for bringing in Saved by the Belle in particular. At least he hoped he'd tempered that not-so-noble motive by emphasizing what it had been about Mariah that made her uniquely qualified to help Robin: she was a real lady, could teach the girl the best qualities of that kind of woman.

Yet as it turned out, the social worker hadn't mentioned in her report that well-intentioned reasoning, either. He wondered why. It didn't quite make sense.

He also wondered how her report might have changed had he taken Mariah up on her offer of marriage. Himself, he'd have thought it would look pretty fishy, too much as if he were still trying to come up with a quick fix to any deficiencies in his abilities.

But in his heart, Jeb knew that if Mariah had said she'd loved him, he'd feel quite different about everything right now. Regardless of how it looked, he'd have felt, with Mariah by his side, that he truly had a chance, and not merely at keeping Robin. For it would have become a matter not of him finding a way to thwart Anita's bid for adoption of Robin, or of learning to meet his niece's unique needs, or of providing a maternal influence for the girl. No, it would have been doing all those things *and* achieving his own heart's desire: of being…happy.

Except Mariah hadn't said she loved him. Wanted him, yes—that he knew he had the inside corner on. But loved him? No.

So he'd put all thoughts of her from his mind in order to concentrate on what he should have from the first: securing his adoption of Robin.

After that, though, what would happen? Had he been merely putting Mariah off, telling her that after the hearing perhaps they might have a chance of a relationship together? Agreed, right now was not a choice time to really get to know each other, with so much at stake that might lead them both to do and say things without the best of intentions. But...afterward? As for himself, he knew he would do his damnedest to show her he could make her happy....

The words, so like those he'd said to Anita fourteen years ago, echoed in his head like gunfire. And he should be shot, he figured, for continuing to delude himself with these insane fantasies. Hadn't he learned anything?

Swearing, Jeb restlessly shoved off from the porch railing and nearly mowed Wiley down. Only then did he recall himself to the moment, he'd been so wrapped up in his thoughts.

"Sorry," Jeb mumbled distractedly.

"You've no need to apologize, son. Ever. To me or anyone else."

He glanced up sharply at Wiley's decisive tone, so unlike his easygoing uncle. "Meaning?"

Wiley's answer was forestalled by Lucy galloping up just then, returned from some foraging expedition and darn near turning inside out at finding company up and about this time of night.

The older man stooped to give the dog a pat as he commented in his usual anecdotal way of making a point, "Y'know, when I got you two kids twenty-five years ago, I spent more'n a few sleepless nights myself wonderin' how

I was gonna see to your needs. 'Specially Cody. You—all I seemed to have to do was be there for you, sort of a home base you could range away from, little bit at a time, like a baby bird leavin' the nest. But Cody was a different animal. He needed a whole lot more attention than you did. Blamed near worried me to death I never would be able to provide him with enough of it. Or enough of the right kind.''

With a grunt, Wiley straightened. "I finally decided the best I could do was try to instill in you both a sense of right and wrong, keep you fed and clothed and let nature take its course. And you both seemed to find your way.''

"Yeah, but nature's takin' a whole different course with Robin," Jeb argued. "That's the problem I've been facin' all along—not knowin' what a young woman needs. You know that. I mean, why else would you have called Mariah in the first place?''

"Maybe 'cause I realized I hadn't done as much for you as I should've.''

"What do you mean?''

Wiley scratched four fingernails down a grizzled cheek and shot him a rueful look. "From the very first day you came here, you took such a shine to Texoma and the guide business, and you seemed to belong here. I could've encouraged you more to spread your wings, but I thought, well, maybe you're like me, content with bein' a bachelor and not havin' much more than the lake and a dog for companionship. I sure wasn't going to try to push you out into the world if you weren't inclined to go, just like I wouldn't have held Cody back.''

The night breeze cascaded through the treetops like water over stones. "Problem is," Wiley continued, "I was wrong. Because you're a different animal, too, and as the years've gone by I could tell you haven't been happy here. Or at least not happy alone, even with Robin comin' to live with us and fillin' some of the empty places in us both.''

"It's not your fault, Wiley, if I haven't been happy,''

Jeb assured him. "You did the best by Cody and me you knew how. I've never felt one bit deprived of what mattered most."

"I know that—but do you believe it about yourself? That doing your best for Robin, lettin' her know she'll never lack for love and care no matter where she goes in this world, and that all the rest—the piano instruction or fine clothes or whatever—is just so much window dressing?"

Jeb jammed his fingers into the front pockets of his jeans, hunching his shoulders against the chill of the night. "Yeah, I think I always did believe that, deep down. If not, I certainly learned the lesson good and proper in the past several weeks."

He drew in a lungful of air, letting it out on a sigh as he made himself say, "But the question is, in the final analysis, will the most I have to offer be judged enough?"

"I guess it depends on who's doin' the judging." His uncle studied him solemnly, iron gray eyebrows beetling over keen blue eyes. Jeb stared steadily back.

"We're not talkin' just about what I have to offer Robin, are we, Wiley, or what it is I need to be truly happy?"

"No, I'd say we're not."

Lucy whined, begging for attention, and Jeb dropped to a squat, scratching the dog behind the ears. "Look, I've already let my...situation with Mariah get in the way of concentrating on Robin's happiness."

"Sure, but you had to test the waters to know what was bitin'."

Jeb made a sound of impatience, more with himself than his uncle, even if Wiley's use of pat little proverbs was getting to him. "Yeah, well, I 'tested the waters,' all right—twice—and I haven't had much luck coming up with what I was fishin' for."

"I believe I also taught you what you caught all depended on the bait you used."

"So which is which, then?" he asked as he'd wanted to

those weeks ago when Wiley had bestowed upon him that particular pearl of wisdom. He rose, facing his uncle squarely, knowing he was taking his frustration out on Wiley when it wasn't the older man's fault. None of this was. Whoever Jeb had become, whatever he lacked, the responsibility for it lay at his own feet. "Am I the lure for Mariah, or her for me? Tell me—is it just fate's perverse sense of humor that I fall for that kind of woman, or that the image of a man like me is all they want from me?"

"So do you actually know what it is Mariah wants from you?" Wiley shot back. "What makes you so blamed sure it's somethin' different from what you want from her?"

That brought Jeb up short. Yes, he'd always focused on the differences between them; of course, there were so many of them. They were polar opposites: the good ol' boy and the Southern lady. How could they expect to find any sort of common ground?

And he had reason for caution—he'd laid his heart out to that sort of woman before, only to have her discard it like yesterday's newspaper.

Except Mariah was different from Anita; he'd known it from the first. Not even in the beginning had she treated his concerns and hopes with anything less than respect. She'd never once suggested Robin might be better off with Anita, not even when he'd proposed it himself. She'd always held out her own hope for the best, had always had faith and looked to the possibilities rather than the uncertainties they faced.

Granted, the last suggestion she'd made—that they marry for Robin's sake—had been farfetched as anything he'd ever heard. And yet Mariah must have seen some other redeeming outcome from the proposal, given the mistake she felt she'd made marrying her ex-husband. Something different and redeeming in him, Jeb Albright.

He'd never really told Mariah he loved her, had he? How

could he expect her to give him that validation when he hadn't given her the same?

Jeb glanced over at his uncle. "Looks like I've got some rethinking to do on a couple of subjects, doesn't it?"

Wiley set one large hand on his shoulder and gave it a squeeze. "Son, what's it all about, except that we live 'n' learn." He squinted into the night. "Yep, just live 'n' learn."

Jeb had to smile. He guessed such bromides had become the pearls of wisdom they were because of the truth they contained.

Pearls of wisdom…

Yes, it was time to stop playing the same old somebody-done-me-wrong song and get on with his life. When the hearing was over, he would look Mariah up again, take the time to explore what they had in common without the interference of their insecurities ringing so loudly in their ears. Without them, they might have a chance.

Or was he being naive again—still?

All he knew was he didn't want to spend the rest of his life dreaming about the one he'd let get away.

Chapter Ten

With shaking legs, Mariah climbed the steps to the Grayson County Justice Center in Sherman. For the hundredth time, she wondered if she was making a huge mistake showing up at the adoption hearing uninvited. But she simply couldn't leave the matter as it stood. She wanted—no, *needed*—to provide whatever help and support to Jeb and Robin she could. Certainly she'd made enough of a hash of things by thinking the "personal" services of Saved by the Belle could help those two in the first place, and it was probably best if she didn't compound her failure.

Except, just as she'd been when Jeb had called her out to Texoma to help him find Robin, Mariah was powerless to stay away, no matter what had transpired afterward between her and Jeb. And she *had* been able to help him; perhaps she might do so now. She simply must offer them both whatever support she could, however incomplete, if it would help even the slightest.

Entering the cool interior of the courthouse, Mariah glanced around but saw no one she recognized. Of course, she had come a half hour early, feeling she would need the time to collect her thoughts before she saw Jeb. She had no idea whether she'd be allowed to sit in the courtroom. It didn't matter. She was here; she would stay as long as she was needed.

She nearly dropped her purse while riding the elevator to the second floor courtrooms, her palms were perspiring so. She had no expectation her presence, however well-meaning, would be welcomed. Jeb's expression, the night she'd seen him last, had been so bleak, so determined, so definite. Seeing the ladies' room as she stepped off the elevator, she fled to its sanctuary to pull herself together. She must—for Jeb's sake.

Apparently she was not to have such privacy. The door swishing shut behind her, Mariah came up short at the sight of a stylishly dressed woman standing in front of one of the sinks.

Realizing how odd it would seem if she turned around and left, Mariah crossed to the sink two down from the rest room's only other occupant and rinsed her palms.

They exchanged quick smiles in the mirror, hers absent, the other woman's impersonal. Frowning, Mariah stole another peek. She looked vaguely familiar—something about the softness around her eyes, which was immediately negated by the uncompromising set of her mouth and jaw. Her frosted blond hair was worn short, and looked styled and hair-sprayed to within an inch of its life. Her makeup gave the same impression: not too much, but much too perfect.

Still, barely sparing Mariah a glance, the woman checked her face over, freshening lipstick that hardly needed it. Two gold, intersecting half circles on the side of the clutch resting on the counter designated the bag as Gucci. If Mariah didn't miss her guess, the rest of the woman's ensemble, head to toe, was similarly expensive. And a little overstated, in her opinion—except perhaps for the strand of pearls at the woman's throat that was so like her own, pearls that no proper Southern woman felt dressed without...

Mariah stiffened as realization zinged through her like an electric shock. This woman had to be Anita Babcock. There was the look of Robin about her eyes—yet with none of the girl's sweetness of spirit. But maybe it wasn't Robin's aunt; Mariah had gotten the impression from Jeb that his late sister-in-law and her family had been steeped in Southern tradition. Yet this woman put Mariah more in mind of someone who aspired to such gentility but didn't quite make it. Because it didn't come from inside, where it counted most.

The distinction was both subtle and flagrant, at least to Mariah. For she knew better than anyone that money, privilege and a status life-style did not make either a lady or gentleman.

Was this how Jeb feared Robin would turn out were she allowed to grow up with Anita?

Her thoughts flew back to Jeb's confession that Anita Babcock did not consider him, a redneck bachelor fishing guide, fit to raise her niece—as he considered Anita, an aspiring Southern belle, just as inappropriate. And wasn't she, Mariah, the same kind of woman as Anita?

But no—Jeb had told her that to him, she was a real lady.

There was a clatter, bringing her back to the moment at hand. The woman had dropped her makeup brush into the sink. With a muttered "Excuse me," she scooped it up and crammed the brush and the rest of her makeup into her purse, her hands trembling. Then she whirled around and rushed into one of the lavatory cubicles, banging the door behind her as Mariah stared in amazement.

Why, she had looked nervous as a girl on her first date.

Or a woman seeing an old flame. Or a lover whom she hadn't entirely gotten over.

Then Mariah recalled the evening of Robin's near-accident, Jeb's tortured exclamation echoing in her head: *why* couldn't he have what he wanted most, when Anita had what she'd always wanted out of life?

What had happened between Jeb and Anita? Had she rejected him, was in effect rejecting him again by intervening for custody of their niece? Why, of all the haughty, pretentious, too-good, snobby—

With a clack, Mariah closed her mouth, which had been hanging open, quite uncouthly, as it occurred to her what she could do to really help Jeb Albright.

She turned back to the mirror to give herself a thorough once-over. The cut of her taupe business suit was impeccable, the cream-colored, shawl-collared silk blouse draping perfectly and emphasizing the quality and luminescence of the strand pearls nestled in the indentation at the base of her throat. Out of her own insecurity today, she had abandoned the chaste-looking French braid she had become accustomed to and instead had coiled her hair into her old standby, a twist also of the French variety. It went with the rest of her look: sophisticated, proper, aloof.

She looked every inch a proper Southern lady, right down to the haughty tilt of her chin she realized was more of a front masking self-doubt than any real stuffiness. It was the same, she would wager, for Anita.

Mariah's gaze met her mirrored one, and that doubt assailed her. *Was* she doing this for Jeb's sake, or was her motive really all that noble? What if her hidden agenda made things worse, as it had seemed to do so far? She would never forgive herself—and neither would Jeb.

All she knew was that she had to try.

The woman emerged from the stall, looking no more composed.

"Ms. Babcock?" Mariah said.

She actually jumped. "Yes?"

In her most cultured drawl, Mariah answered, "I was wondering if I might have a word with you."

Anita Babcock gazed at her warily—as warily as Jeb Albright had stared at her the day she'd met him when he'd stood there, Lucy at his side, and looking for all the world like a boy keeping close his best friend for support, uncertain of what sort of reception he should give or would be given.

She was struck now by how vulnerable he'd been, faced with the kind of woman she represented. And yet he'd pressed on, trying to do what he believed he must to see ultimately to the best interests of his niece, regardless of what he was up against in terms of Anita's criticism or personal history with him.

It incensed her that this woman might have treated such a decent, upright man so.

"A talk about what?" Anita asked.

Mariah smiled her sweetest, most sugar-coated smile. "Oh, about certain...ways of conducting oneself two ladies such as ourselves would see eye to eye on."

Yes, she and Anita Babcock were going to have a little talk, Southern belle to Southern belle.

As Wiley followed, Jeb ushered his niece ahead of him into the austere interior of the courthouse. Robin still managed to keep hold of his hand, like a little girl fearful of getting lost, and Jeb gave her fingers a squeeze of reassurance. He knew the feeling. They were all forging deep into unfamiliar waters. Now he knew why he'd always preferred to remain in the surroundings of Texoma. He felt completely out of his element here, unlearned in the ways of this environment and therefore vulnerable.

Ken Montgomery, his lawyer, was already waiting upstairs. Nearby stood a man Jeb recognized from Cody and Lisa's funeral as Randy Babcock, Anita's husband. Arms crossed, he was talking in low tones to another man who had to be their lawyer. Both looked as if they'd stepped out of a magazine article headlined "How to Dress like a Million Bucks." They exuded power, control and experience.

Jeb smoothed down his tie. Both his suit and Wiley's had been bought new for his brother's funeral; neither Jeb nor his uncle had had need of such formal attire up till then, or need of it in the future, so they hadn't exactly shot a wad on the clothes. Still, Jeb hadn't thought they looked half-bad until he saw the other two men.

He felt Wiley's hand cuff him around the collar. "Remember, son," the older man said, "just 'cause you put your boots in the oven, that don't make 'em biscuits."

Jeb threw him a thankful smile. It was another of Wiley's little sayings: in other words, clothes didn't make the man—either himself, or Randy Babcock and his lawyer.

"There you are!" A smiling Cathy Sperry came down the hall from the courtroom. "Don't you look nice today, Robin," she commented warmly as she reached them.

"Th-thank you," the girl answered automatically. She did look nice, Jeb thought, in a Western-blouse-and-culottes set, opaque tights and a pair of popular lace-up boots that were feminine but still exactly Robin's style. On her clothes he'd spared no expense. He'd helped her with her hair, worn loose today except for the barrette Mariah had given her holding back the top section in the back, and she hadn't balked a bit on any of his recommendations. She knew it would be to his benefit for her to look every inch the well-taken-care-of girl. The long sleeves of the blouse hid the healing scrape on her forearm.

The social worker put an arm around Robin's shoulders. "Why don't you come with me and I'll find us a place to sit together?'' However politely phrased, it was not a request.

Robin looked to him, shadows in her blue eyes, perhaps wondering as he was if their time together was up. Her fate would be sealed inside this courthouse today. Whom would she walk out with—him or Anita?

''Go on, girl,'' he said with another squeeze of her hand. She nodded and allowed herself to be led away.

It wouldn't be the end of the world if Robin was awarded to Anita, Jeb told himself. It wouldn't. He'd still be able to visit her, have her come visit him and Wiley.

But as he watched her walk away, he felt his very heartstrings unraveling.

Ken spotted him and gave him a nervous smile as Jeb and Wiley made their way over. ''Let's see if we can get your adoption of your niece wrapped up and in the bag,'' Ken said in his best confident-attorney voice.

''Then I think we'd better be prepared to swim with the sharks,'' Jeb murmured dryly with a surreptitious inclination of his head in the direction of the opposing attorney.

''I've noticed.'' Ken shifted his briefcase to his other hand. ''You should have let me hire a P.I. to nose around and see what we could've come up with on the Babcocks. You've got to know they did their own snooping around.''

''I told you, Ken, I'm not going to play that game.''

The lawyer looked askance at the other attorney. ''I don't exactly approve of such tactics myself, but it sure would be nice to have an ace in the hole right now, for security's sake if nothing else.'' His lips thinned as he set his mouth. ''I guarantee I'll do my very best for you today, Jeb.''

Jeb clapped the other man on the shoulder. ''I know you will, Ken. That's all I can expect.''

As he had from the first, Jeb liked the guy's sincerity, even if he had an idea money bought more justice these days than righteousness did. He'd hired Ken six months

ago to deal with what was to have been a fairly straight-
forward adoption, given the biological relation between him
and Robin. Adoptions of any kind, he had learned quickly
when shopping legal counsel, came at quite a price. Ken
had been young, eager and cheap.

Jeb realized now he probably should have sought the
advice of a more experienced lawyer once Anita had come
forward to intervene, even if it put him up to his ears in
debt, because from the looks of her attorney, both he and
Ken were way out of their league.

"Well, I think we've got as good a chance as the other
side," Ken said, then lowered his voice and went on, "We
really caught a break when the social worker didn't include
that incident with the down-rigger in her report. Now, if
we can just keep a positive slant on the situation with Saved
by the Belle."

"Whoa, there!" Wiley gave Jeb a nudge. "Speakin' of
which."

Jeb turned to see Mariah Duncan emerge from the ladies'
room on the other side of the building. She paused just
outside the door as if composing herself, while he drank in
the sight of her as a thirsting man would water.

She had such power to take his breath away, looking
refined and classy, and pale and elegant as a magnolia blos-
som. He'd never seen her with her hair up like that, making
her look as if she belonged on the arm of a Southern blue
blood comparable to herself.

Then she spotted him, her lips curving into a smile as
she started toward him, giving him an opportunity to look
at her shapely legs extending from the hem of her above-
the-knee slim skirt to her beige high-heeled pumps. He remembered those legs wrapping around his waist, and it
hardly seemed that moment could have been real, seeing
her now.

God, she was so beautiful. So out of his league.

"Hello, Jeb," she said, reaching him, doe eyes warm and caring and calm, as if fired with an inner conviction, warming him, too.

"Hello, Mariah," Jeb managed to say, shoving his hands in his pockets to keep from yanking her into his arms in front of everybody. But Ken and Wiley, even Randy Babcock and his lawyer, had moved away. "I sure didn't expect to see you here today."

"I had to come, try to help however I could."

He was unaccountably touched. "I appreciate the moral support."

"I hope to…wish I might do more." She touched the pearls at her throat with two fingertips, the gesture seeming different to him this time, though still a reminder of some kind. "It's only now occurred to me how I could provide you with the kind of help I've wanted to all along. The kind of service, even, that Saved by the Belle advertised it could provide."

"Yes, well, Ken and I decided it would be too risky, calling you to testify," he explained. "We didn't want the other side getting more chance than necessary to twist around my hiring you into a not very swift attempt to compensate for my limited experience and resources," he finished with a wry lift of one side of his mouth.

Her focus zeroed in on his uneven smile, then returned to his eyes. "I understand," she said softly. And looking into her tender brown gaze, Jeb believed she truly did.

"Mariah," he said huskily, "this probably isn't the best time for me to say this—I don't know that there ever will be—but I've finally decided I can't let what's happened in the past keep me from going after what I want to make me hap—"

A flash of color at the periphery of his vision distracted him. Glancing up, he saw a woman in red and gold come out the same door Mariah had a moment before. Almost like radar, her gaze homed in on Jeb and locked. *Anita.*

Thoughts of what he'd been about to say evaporated as they stared at each other, almost a sizing up of the competition. He didn't know how he came off to her. As for himself, he'd have liked to wonder what he ever saw in her, but the signs of his old attraction were there: the fascinating contrast of that polished shell with an inquisitive sensuality lurking just beneath it; the determined focus that, as long as you were its target, could be downright exhilarating.

She had changed, though. Gone was a certain youthful expectancy. An innocence. She definitely didn't wear the look he'd have thought a woman would who had gotten everything she'd ever wanted out of life.

Well, if she hadn't, he at least—no, thank heaven—wasn't to blame. He guessed the Garth Brooks song was right, in that some of God's greatest gifts were unanswered prayers.

Steadily he maintained Anita's gaze. She was the first to glance away as she straightened her shoulders and stalked down the hall and into the courtroom.

But not before he saw the look of recognition—and something else—pass between her and Mariah.

Jeb's stomach catapulted into his throat. That look…as if they understood each other perfectly—in a way he never would.

And what had Mariah said, something about Saved by the Belle helping in the way it really could?

Oh, *had* he been incredibly gullible?

"What's going on here, Mariah?" Jeb demanded.

Apparently she'd recognized the unfavorable impression he'd been given, which only reinforced his doubt. "It's not what you think," she asserted, laying her hand on his arm.

Ken poked his head out of the courtroom. "Jeb, we need to get going here."

"In a minute," Jeb told him, turning back to Mariah. "What did you mean about Saved by the Belle helping me?"

"Maybe I should have cleared it with you first, but—"

"Jeb, the bailiff's two seconds from announcing the judge," Ken interrupted. "I'd like us not to be running for our places like a couple of schoolboys when Her Honor comes into the room."

"I'm comin'." Jeb didn't move, though, but searched the depths of Mariah's gaze with his own. She didn't falter one bit.

"Trust me, Jeb," she whispered.

He just shook his head, doubt more than denial, and drew his arm away from her touch.

And still she didn't hesitate. "Trust yourself, too."

"Jeb," Ken warned nervously.

"I guess I'll have to," Jeb muttered, turning from Mariah and striding into the courtroom.

With a deep breath, he took his seat next to Ken and tried to put all thoughts of Mariah aside, though they continued to overrun his mind. Damn him for once again letting himself become distracted! If he lost Robin through his own ignorance and shortsightedness, he would never forgive himself.

The hearing began.

The judge was Irene Dorchester—a woman, which, Ken had told Jeb, was a mild strike against them. But Ken said the midfiftyish judge had been a resident of the Texoma area her entire life; in other words, she was closer to being Jeb's kind of folks than Anita's.

Except Judge Dorchester wore pearls with her black robes.

As he was the original petitioner, Jeb's side of the case

was presented first. Ken called to the stand Arthur Underwood, who was able, as a client of Jeb's and an officer at the bank the Albrights had always used, to give an outstanding account of Jeb's character and citizenship. Similarly glowing testimony was given by Robin's school counselor, as well as by two of her playmates' mothers, one with whom Jeb had attended high school. Next came Wiley, who charmed the judge and touched everyone's hearts with his down-home recollections of raising his two orphaned nephews on Texoma. The parallel to Jeb's situation with Robin was played to the hilt.

It was looking good for them, very good, Ken told them at lunch break, while still cautioning Jeb and Wiley that the Babcocks would be putting their best foot forward, too, when their turn came. He was kind of surprised that Paul Harrison, the attorney for the Babcocks, hadn't seriously undermined the testimony in cross-examination so far. It had Ken a little worried, but he wasn't going to look a gift horse in the mouth.

Jeb, however, had noticed the Jaws-like gleam in the other lawyer's eye and wondered if they were all being incredibly naive. Strangely, despite his unexpressed doubts about Mariah's appearance here today, he found her presence in the courtroom reassuring. It was very hard for him to keep up his defenses—against her, at least.

The afternoon proceeded in a similarly favorable fashion—until Ken announced, "Your Honor, I'd like to call Mr. Jeb Albright to the stand."

Jeb rose and was sworn in. He and Ken had run through the questions the lawyer would be asking him, centering primarily on how he had from the beginning stepped forward to take responsibility for his niece, had applied for adoption of her at his earliest opportunity and had always demonstrated his desire to do his best for Robin.

Then came the tricky part.

"And so in your endeavor to see to your niece's particular needs," Ken said, "you hired Mariah Duncan, a professional organizer who advertised the services of her business, Saved by the Belle, as providing individual client attention 'with a Southern touch.'"

"Yes, I did," Jeb answered. They had decided to describe Mariah's involvement in their own words, believing that to leave out all mention of Saved by the Belle would have invited speculation that Jeb's motives might not have been altogether conscientious. And since Cathy Sperry hadn't explained his reasons for hiring Mariah in her report, Jeb and Ken had thought it best to expand upon it in testimony.

"What service was Ms. Duncan to provide you and your niece?"

"Well, seein' as I'd been raised in pretty much an all-male and kind of rough environment, I felt I needed some advice on how to raise a girl up proper…ly." He reached up to ease a finger under the stiff collar of his shirt, then remembered Ken's caution not to fidget while on the stand, which could make him appear to be hiding something.

But he had nothing to hide—or at least nothing that misrepresented what and who he was. His gaze involuntarily strayed to Mariah, fastened on those doe eyes that asked him to trust.

"And what sort of things did you and Ms. Duncan do to work toward this aim?"

Dragging his attention back, Jeb clasped his hands to still them, elbows propped on the arms of his chair. "Mariah helped me take Robin shopping for some feminine clothes. She was there to make suggestions for redecorating Robin's room, you know, to make it more to Robin's taste and liking. We enrolled her in piano lessons and encouraged her to participate in activities with her friends. Oh, and Mariah advised me on the particular needs and issues of a girl who was growing fast into a young lady,'' he explained with nary a blush and not one bit of hesitation as he focused on his niece.

"Did you find that particular situation uncomfortable?"

"A little—until I found a way to relate to Robin in my own way. But I was committed to doing whatever it took to see to her happiness and well-being.''

The girl's blue eyes shone with love and dedication. Then his focus shifted again to Mariah, where she sat directly behind Robin and Ms. Sperry.

And some impulse compelled him to go on without prompting, "Mostly, though, I'd realized it wasn't fair to deprive Robin of half her background, if I could at all prevent that from happening. I might be able to give her a sense of her father and the influence Cody might have been on her had he lived, but I knew I wasn't going to come near to keepin' Lisa alive in Robin's mind. And I wanted that for her. For...both of them.''

His gaze now lit on Anita, for she was staring at him, motionless except for a slight trembling of her mouth. For the first time, Jeb saw the girl he'd fallen for all those years ago.

Glancing away, he cleared his throat, knowing he must be absolutely truthful. "Problem was, I didn't see myself as marrying the kind of woman Lisa had been. So, even on a temporary basis, Mariah Duncan seemed the closest I could provide, because...''

He saw the caution in Ken's expression that he not make comparisons, not paint himself in less than the best light— or into a corner. Jeb wondered why he *did* continue to speak, for he had no guarantee whatever had passed between Mariah and Anita wouldn't be his downfall. But quite simply he saw it as his responsibility to tell the truth, a truth he still believed in.

Trust me—trust yourself, too, Mariah had whispered. The conviction was in her soulful eyes right now.

"Because," Jeb said, "Mariah Duncan's what I call a real lady."

As always when he used those words, Mariah stiffened as if taking a blow. He'd always been puzzled before by that reaction, a reaction similar to his when he was categorized as a simple rural man. Now, though, it struck him how the image—both his and hers—could fall on either side of the fence, depending on who was making the distinction.

How could he have failed to see that aspect before?

Then he noticed the encouragement radiating from Cathy Sperry and knew why she'd omitted some of his reasoning from her report. He needed to say this here, now.

"What I mean is," Jeb continued, looking directly into the brown-eyed gaze of the woman he loved, "I saw a lot of the qualities in Mariah I saw in Robin's mother—a thoughtfulness and quiet consideration in her dealings with others. Sort of a...Southern gentility that comes from some inner store of strength and wisdom and integrity. Even if Lisa hadn't had those qualities in her, I couldn't see how they would ever be bad ones for Robin to learn, and learn to be respected for."

Now he did redden in earnest, sure he sounded as absurd and inarticulate as Jethro Bodine reciting Shakespeare. Except he noticed how Mariah's troubled expression had changed, like morning conquering the night, to one of loving appreciation—almost as if he had given her a precious gift. The greatest gift he could give her: his utmost respect for who she was.

How that look leapt through him, as if some divine vision smote him and filled him with such...happiness.

Apparently recognizing a good curtain line when he

heard one, Ken murmured, "No more questions, Your Honor."

Jeb was brought out of his reverie and back to the matter at hand by Judge Dorchester saying, "Your witness, Mr. Harrison."

The fair-haired lawyer stood in a leisurely manner. Jeb wasn't fooled.

Harrison smiled benignly. "Mr. Albright, you just stated you felt less than qualified to raise a girl 'properly,' given your particular environment, occupation and personal history."

"Yes," Jeb answered forthrightly enough.

"And that was why you hired Ms. Duncan—because she would be able to provide you guidance in raising your niece to a...gentler existence?"

"Yes."

"As you saw your late sister-in-law providing for her daughter before her untimely death."

"Along with my brother's own individual perspective as Robin's father," Jeb agreed with an innocuous smile of his own.

"Yes, of course." Harrison pressed the outside edge of one index finger against his pursed lips in a pose of apparent deliberation. "Yet you did believe that sort of upbringing—very much how my client, Mrs. Babcock, was raised—was in a sense better than what you could offer Robin?"

Jeb raised a skeptical eyebrow. "Not exactly."

"I see. Could the situation have been you had a quite personal and not altogether selfless reason for feeling you must do, in your words—" he consulted his notes "—'whatever it took' to retain custody of Robin?"

"What I said was I'd do whatever it took to see to her happiness."

"A happiness, in your perception, that included the influence of a woman like Lisa Albright. The kind of woman, you said, you did not see yourself as being able to marry."

"Yes," Jeb said warily, sensing what was coming but seeing no way to stop it.

"Is it not true, Mr. Albright, that fourteen years ago you had a romantic relationship with Mrs. Babcock and that she rejected your offer of marriage?"

"Objection, Your Honor," Ken spoke up. "Irrelevant."

"Overruled," the judge decreed. "You may answer, Mr. Albright."

With effort Jeb held the attorney's gaze, refusing to glance away even as his heart pounded against his ribs. He'd hoped this point wouldn't come up, for Robin's sake. Hoped that Anita and—Jeb admitted his part—he himself would not let this deteriorate into a grudge match, clouding the focus of what should be their foremost concern: a little girl's happiness.

He must remember that was what lay at stake here, even if he would stand up for himself and who he was.

From the periphery of his vision, Jeb saw Anita drop her gaze, either unwilling or unable to look at him. Saw Mariah's noticeable study of his old lover, although from here he couldn't tell what her exact expression might reveal about her thoughts. He couldn't believe what a disaster this was all turning out to be, one in which he stood to lose not only his niece, but the regard of the woman he loved.

It wouldn't happen! he vowed. Somehow, some way, he'd hold on to them both.

"Yes," he answered with dead calm.

"And you've never married, Mr. Albright?"

"Nope."

"So can you truthfully say Mrs. Babcock's rejection hasn't had its lingering effect upon you?"

"If you mean does my petition to adopt Robin have anything to do with getting back a bit of my own from a four-

teen-year-old spurning, you'll recall I'm not doing the intervening here.''

Ken gave him a private grin of congratulations for turning the tables on that line of questioning.

Harrison did not appear disconcerted. ''Let's go back to
the issue of your feeling the environment you would be
raising Robin in as being less than ideal, shall we, Mr.
Albright? And in hiring Saved by the Belle you were just
trying to do your best by your niece, am I right?''

Jeb knew a bait-and-switch tactic when he came upon
one. ''Yes,'' he said, wondering what dangerous waters this
tack would lead him into.

''How well do you believe you and Ms. Duncan succeeded in your plan to better equip you to handle Robin's
specific needs?''

''I wouldn't call it an unqualified success, but I wouldn't
say it was a total loss, not at all.'' He didn't flinch under
the attorney's sharp scrutiny. He just wished he knew what
had really passed between Mariah and Anita. ''We all
learned some valuable lessons—about ourselves, about
life.''

''Then why sever your relationship with Saved by the
Belle, as you did a full month ago? Unless your scheme's
detrimental effect on Robin outweighed any strides made
with her.''

''No,'' he contradicted, wondering what Mariah *had* told
Anita, if anything, about their own relationship with each
other, a relationship that distracted them both from their
goals, which had essentially been the reason he and Mariah
had decided to part ways. ''Mariah and I agreed that while
we'd made progress, Robin and I were doing just fine on
our own.''

''Meaning you felt perfectly capable of seeing to Robin's
upbringing without outside assistance from even a surrogate
feminine figure?''

"Perfectly capable? No, I didn't feel that at all. But I am what I am, Mr. Harrison. I may marry eventually, but for now I'm on my own and I was going to need to raise Robin with the values I'd been raised with—learning right from wrong, always striving to do your best, treating people how you'd like to be treated and being true to yourself. It was enough for me—and I've come to believe it's enough for any kid, boy or girl."

"A noble sentiment, Mr. Albright. But let's explore whether what you have to offer your niece by way of guidance *is* enough."

The man narrowed his eyes, looking for all the world like a predator circling for the kill, and even though he'd been expecting it, Jeb found himself hit broadside.

"For example," the attorney asked with ferocious directness, "tell the court why Robin nearly came to disastrous harm on the evening of May thirtieth when she caught her sleeve in the cable of the down-rigger on your fishing boat."

Chapter Eleven

Mariah saw all color drain from Jeb's face, as she felt it do from her own. Then his laser blue eyes cut to her, bore into her, searching. And hurting, as if he'd been cut to the quick. The question in his eyes was, *Is this your doing?*

She shook her head in answer, completely appalled at the turn of events, the worst that could happen for Jeb. She noticed Cathy Sperry doing the same.

It didn't matter where the Babcocks had gotten the information; it was out now. Mariah felt her heart thud sickeningly. How was Jeb to recover from this development?

Her gaze shot to Anita, who sat staring at her lap, features taut with pain, acting for all the world as if this attack on Jeb hurt her more than it hurt him. Mariah wanted to scream at her. *Didn't you hear a word I said?* Was the woman really so cold, so unfeeling?

God help me, Mariah thought, if I have anything in common with Anita Babcock.

"Robin came away with a scrape on her arm, that's all," Jeb responded firmly.

"Yet it could have been much worse, could it not?" Harrison parried, going for the throat. "According to J. T. Hicks, from J.T.'s Boat Repair, you told him in passing that Robin had been lucky not to have lost a finger—or worse."

"Objection, Your Honor," Ken Montgomery broke in forcefully. "Hearsay."

"Sustained." The judge removed her glasses and set them on top of her notes. "Though I would be interested in hearing, Mr. Albright, what actually did happen."

Firing the opposing attorney a lethal look, one Mariah wouldn't have wanted to have aimed at her, Jeb said calmly, "Robin was just wanting to…to belong, except my bringing in Mariah Duncan to sort of spruce us both up made her feel the opposite, like the more different she was from Wiley and me, the less we'd want her to remain with us on Texoma. Or that I might get to thinking girls were too much trouble to have around. That wasn't true, not one bit, but I'd told her a story a few days before about how her father had liked to tinker with things, and when she saw the trouble I was having with the down-rigger, she thought to try and fix it, sort of take her daddy's place and fit in to our family."

His Adam's apple bobbed, and Mariah saw Jeb clench his jaw to contain his emotions. But he would have the truth told. "The fact of the matter is, I should have known what Robin was going through, and my getting sidetracked is what caused the near-accident. I'll make no bones about my part in that."

"And given that, how could you even remotely still believe that Robin is better off with you than with the Babcocks?" Harrison drove his point home. "Remember, now, you've sworn you want only the best for your niece."

Jeb hesitated, and Mariah had never seen him so at war with himself. It wasn't right, to make this honest, upright man feel this way—that who and what he was were not enough.

Mariah shook her head, her eyes stinging. No, it wasn't right at all. Sparing not another half a second thinking of what she might be doing, she sprang to her feet. "Your Honor, the incident with the down-rigger *wasn't* Mr. Albright's fault, it was mine."

All attention was riveted on her, and for a moment everyone was too stunned to speak, which Mariah took advantage of. "Jeb had only been following my advice. If I hadn't made the error of selling my services to them as some sort of miracle-working Southern belle, when that wasn't the kind of help they needed at all, then Robin wouldn't have been made to feel alienated."

"Your Honor," Harrison quickly interjected, "I am trying to question the witness here."

Jeb promptly spoke up, "Yeah, and I want to make it clear Mariah was only doing what she'd said she could do. I was the one who was blind to what was going on."

Mariah wanted to hug him and hit him at the same time.

The judge's gavel banged down as she frowned mightily. She had barely opened her mouth to reprimand them when another contradiction rang out in the courtroom.

"It was my fault!" Robin stood, clutching the back of the seat in front of her. "Totally. I'll swear it on a Bible."

"Your honor, please," Harrison said impatiently.

"I was the one who was messin' around with something I shouldn't have," Robin rushed on. She looked about to cry, but from somewhere within her she found the strength to continue. "Uncle Jeb taught me all the rules of how to act around boats and equipment. He knows his stuff, and he wouldn't let anyone get into a fishin' situation that was over their heads."

The judge again tried to regain order. "This is completely out of line, young lady."

Robin stood fast. "Uncle Jeb's *never* treated me like I couldn't be part of the family 'cause I was a girl."

Though her voice was cracking, she managed to go on with eloquence, "Judge... Your Honor. If you decide I have to go live with Aunt Anita, I will. But not because y'all think my uncle Jeb's just a redneck fishing guide who doesn't know how to deal with girls. He's not, you know. It was me who wasn't... who didn't..."

Robin couldn't finish, breaking down completely. In the next instant, Jeb sprang from his chair on the witness stand, out of order or not, coming to the aid of his niece. As was Mariah. She had rounded the end of the bench seat and reached Robin just as her uncle did.

Four arms reached out to comfort the girl, and Mariah found her hug encompassing Jeb, as his comforting clasp included her, too. Oh, to feel those strong arms about her again! Over Robin's head, their glances collided. Connected. Mariah read the doubts about her that continued to linger in Jeb's transparent blue eyes, and she almost cried. Then she saw also the struggle to trust and have faith, despite evidence to the contrary, despite past experiences that gave him more than enough reason to be wary.

His arm tightened about her waist, pulling her closer and into the circle of his protective embrace.

By now everyone in the courtroom was on their feet, both lawyers leaping to the defense of their clients and taking full advantage of this opportunity to undermine their opponent.

The judge pounded her gavel. "Order—*now!*"

The courtroom quieted instantly, and Judge Dorchester's gimlet gaze made a circuit of the assemblage. She drew herself up. "Ms. Duncan, you are out of order. You, too, Robin. We'll have no further outbursts." Her gaze softened as she said to the girl, "You'll have your chance in chambers to tell me anything you think I should know. And, Mr.

Albright, you will return to the stand and answer only those questions addressed to you.''

However, none of them moved as Robin and Mariah continued to cling to Jeb, standing tall and noble as a Southern statesman from the past.

The judge looked from the small cohesive knot they made to Anita, who still had done nothing, said nothing.

Judge Dorchester shook her head and commented dryly, "Why is it I am beginning to feel like King Solomon?"

Perhaps unwisely, given the judge's still-grim expression, but suddenly feeling she, too, was filled with the conviction of another age, Mariah spoke up again. "That might be, Your Honor, because it's evident from what just happened here that Jeb Albright has what it takes to inspire great love and loyalty in people, and it's because he holds the happiness of those he loves above all other considerations and doesn't take that responsibility lightly. And that's what really counts in a parent, right?''

Down came the gavel with a resounding crack. Sure enough, Judge Dorchester had not taken kindly to the disruption, however well-meaning or politely phrased. "Ms. Duncan, you leave me no choice but to have you escorted from the courtroom. Bailiff!"

The uniformed man started toward her. Impossibly—thrillingly—Jeb's hold upon Mariah grew even more snug, his jaw turning to steel along with his eyes, resting upon the advancing officer of the court. And she perceived just what it meant to be loved by this unassuming rural man. It was all she'd ever wanted. But she knew she must be up to that kind of love.

She might as well go for broke.

In a way that no proper Southern woman ever would conduct herself, Mariah confronted Anita head-on.

"Don't you even begin to think that this man will be without a mother for Robin forever," she said, adhering to him with her arms about his neck as the bailiff made to pry her away from Jeb. She had to get this out before she let herself be ejected from the courtroom, which she would allow; she wouldn't be the cause of a physical confrontation between Jeb and the bailiff, which would probably result in both she and Jeb being held in contempt. "If he hasn't married already it's through no fault of his own but because of the women who wouldn't know a real catch if it jumped up and bit them on the nose. Because Jeb Albright's the genuine article!"

The bailiff had finally managed to lock on to one of her arms. Jeb in turn grabbed the bailiff's wrist, and Robin looked ready to get into the act as Mariah watched in horror the girl raising one stylish boot, about to bring it down upon the poor man's instep.

The whole scene had the makings of a kicker bar free-for-all. Oh, if Stephen and her society friends could see her now!

"Wait!"

All heads turned. Anita Babcock stood, shaking visibly. "I...I..." she stammered.

"Yes, Mrs. Babcock?" the judge prompted with a huge sigh.

"I...I would like to hear Jeb's answer to my attorney's question—h-how he believes Robin would be better off with him."

Judge Dorchester treated them all to a glare that said she was this close to tossing the lot of them from the court-room, but acceded to Anita's request and motioned to the bailiff to let Mariah stay for the moment. "Mr. Albright, you may answer."

The courtroom fell silent as Jeb's searching scrutiny probed for the truth in his ex-lover's eyes.

"I'll admit it," he said. "I'm a simple man raised with-out much for feminine influence. I lost my mother, and my father, when I was just a kid. And more important than gender, we have that in common, Robin and me—that loss of trust and innocence and a little bit of ourselves, too, that can never be recovered."

Harrison opened his mouth, apparently intending to cut off any more of Jeb's heartfelt disclosure, but Anita stayed the attorney with a gesture, her face a study of mixed emotions.

Jeb seemed not to notice; his eyes were on Robin, who stared up at him, lashes still spiky with her shed tears. "I understand better than anyone, just as she understands the same about me, the insecurity of constantly wonderin' if you'd ever belong, if you'd ever be enough."

He shrugged, that same gesture of acceptance Mariah had seen before; now, though, she saw another kind of acceptance, one that did not apologize. "But even with that burden to shoulder, I've learned you can still be trustful, still look to the possibilities in life and have faith."

Mariah noticed his voice had lost nearly all of its backwoods twang as he spoke from his heart. The kind of man he was, *was* enough, because in that heart lay conviction, durable and enduring as the bois d'arc tree.

She gave him an encouraging squeeze, though he little needed it as he went on, "And so I do believe in my unique ability to provide Robin with a standard of how to live her life, one that'll stand her in good stead wherever she goes in this world."

Then Mariah found herself the recipient of Jeb's laser blue gaze, searching and surrendering, and she caught her breath at the emotion in his eyes, for she saw he believed, too, in his ability to give her what she really needed to be happy, if she would but give him the chance.

Their faces were inches apart, and Mariah was quite certain she would be unable to restrain herself from kissing him right in front of everyone.

"If the court will allow me a minute with my client," Harrison said in response to Anita's murmured comment to him.

Everyone waited as, chin held high and hands clasped resolutely in her lap, Anita sat between her husband and their lawyer, both of whom bent their heads together to hear what she was saying. Harrison appeared to be arguing vehemently.

Anita shook her head no, again and again.

Finally the attorney rose and said with great forbearance, "Your Honor. My clients wish to withdraw their intervention at this time. We do not contest Mr. Albright's petition for adoption."

A collective stunned gasp echoed through the courtroom as relief washed over Mariah, for she knew that, indeed, she had not been wrong: she and Anita understood each other perfectly.

The judge sat back in her leather chair, rolling her pearls between thumb and forefinger, her mouth pursed as she seemed to think through the chain of events in her courtroom today. "Ms. Sperry," she said at last, addressing the social worker she had appointed, "does your recommendation for Jeb Albright still hold, given the circumstances that have come to light?"

"Yes, Your Honor." Cathy Sperry nodded definitely. "In fact, I was there in the aftermath of the down-rigger incident."

The judge's eyebrows rose a full inch. "Indeed. We've worked together many years, Ms. Sperry, so I've no concerns you haven't taken due care in doing your job. I'm simply not sure you've taken the same care in remembering your position."

She made a few notes, apparently oblivious that the room was full of people hanging on her every word.

"Very well," she proclaimed. "The court awards adoption of Robin Albright to her uncle, Jeb Albright."

She closed the case file with a snap as the bailiff called, "All rise!"

No one moved for several seconds after the judge left the courtroom. Her heart near to bursting, Mariah watched Jeb bend his cheek to the crown of Robin's head in silent thanks.

"Jeb."

He glanced up. Anita had come forward alone. She held out her hand in a gesture of goodwill. Relinquishing his hold on both his niece and Mariah, he took it.

"I was right about you all along, you know," she said with a watery smile. "I was the one who wasn't...the genuine article, shall we say." Her voice dropped. "I'm sorry for the pain I've caused you. You deserved better from me."

"I've no reason to hold a grudge, Anita. We've both got what we wanted, haven't we?"

Her lashes fell as a flash of pain crossed her features, and Mariah actually found within herself sympathy for the other woman. But then, such was Southern graciousness.

Anita reached out to stroke her fingers through her niece's hair. "Robin, you know I want only the best for you, don't you?"

Mariah watched proudly as the girl gave her aunt a compassionate smile wise beyond her years. "I *am* getting the best, Aunt Anita."

"Will you come visit us in Houston, now that we're putting down roots there?"

"Sure." She shot Mariah a quick glance. "I mean, thank you, I'd like that very much, Aunt Anita."

Anita actually laughed, although the sound was tinged with sadness. She cupped Robin's chin, and the girl looked up at her with those clear blue eyes. "Dear girl," Anita whispered. "You are so very much like both your parents, you know."

She took a fortifying breath. "Well. I hope I'll be seeing you soon, Robin. Until then, goodbye." Her gaze lingered on Jeb. "Goodbye, Jeb."

Mariah saw his own clear-eyed gaze rest on the woman he'd once risked all and proposed marriage to, and her throat constricted in sudden doubt. He'd been hurt so badly by Anita. Would he actually want to get involved with another woman who from most appearances had so little in common with him?

Mariah couldn't tell from the way he nodded and said, "Goodbye, Anita."

After her aunt left, Robin noticed Mariah and Jeb's sudden awkwardness. With her usual perceptiveness, the girl announced, "Gosh, I haven't given Uncle Wiley a hug!"

That left Jeb and Mariah alone.

"So," she said brightly, "I guess this means I'll be able to obtain a reference from you."

Jeb stuck his hands in his trouser pockets. "No doubt about it, I was saved by the belle."

Mariah concentrated on straightening her purse strap, uncertain whether he meant her or Anita.

He lifted her chin with one finger beneath it. "What did you say to her, Mariah?"

"We just had a little talk, Southern belle to Southern belle, that's all."

"And?"

Mariah gave an impatient sigh but saw no way not to answer him truthfully. Not when he demanded her complete honesty with his eyes. "*And* I told her I knew what she saw when she looked at Jeb Albright—a man of limited resources who, because of his restricted experiences and background as a bachelor fishing guide living out in the country, might seem rather ignorant of what it takes to make a woman happy. But you see, Jeb, I was married for six years to a man who had the proper upbringing and all the trappings of fine gentleman, and he knew nothing about what a woman really wants—or needs.''

His eyes widened. ''And what's that?''

''Jeb. You've always known. That's what I told Anita. That you're no ordinary man. You're good and noble and, yes, maybe a little artless. But you have…vision, is the only way I could think to put it. A vision of how you should conduct yourself and how to treat others, a vision of what you're due from others in return, that has never wavered. And because of that, you're the best parent a girl could have. The best man any woman could wish for.''

She knew her heart was in her eyes but there was no holding back, no caution left in her. ''And that, if you ask me, is what I call the real deal, the genuine article. Anita Babcock had her chance, and she blew it. She knows she did, because, Jeb Albright, you're real marriage material. I'm not going to make the mistake Anita did by not seeing the diamond in the rough, the heart of gold beneath the rugged exterior. In fact, I…I'd like to ask again if you'll marry me.''

He said nothing, but oh, those beautiful eyes of his were as always stripped bare of any protection, laying his own heart open to her. She smiled, drawing a half smile in answer from him, a hesitant one. Then she saw what made him so—disbelief, the kind that was wondering how it could happen to him, a simple man such as himself, that the best and most cherished of his dreams was coming true.

Her heart swelled painfully in her chest, at once aching for the hurt and loss he had suffered in the past and relief of that ache through the love she gave him.

Then the other half of his mouth stretched to match the turned-up side to make a perfect, full-out grin.

''You mean it?'' he asked.

"I purely do."

"Then I guess I'd be next door to a philistine not to take you up on your offer."

He got the wildest look in his eyes as he pulled her into his arms. It thrilled her to her bones. "You do know, though, what it'll be like bein' married to me," he drawled in that sexy twang.

"Oh, yes. And I am so looking forward to it."

He kissed her then with that barely leashed, barely civilized urgency, and she hung on to his lapels and kissed him back with the same fervor.

"I do love you, Jeb," Mariah said against his lips.

"I love you, too, M'riah. You truly won't mind bein' the wife of a redneck fishin' guide?"

"Not if you can put up with a certified Southern belle."

"But you're not a Southern belle," he said seriously. "You're not actually a real lady, either. I'd have to say, you're a true Southern...woman."

She kissed him again for giving her that. For knowing the difference. It was more than enough for them to have in common.

They looked up to find Wiley and Robin grinning at them.

"Hey there, Robbie," Jeb said, tucking Mariah against one side to make room for his niece on the other, "what do you say to getting a new dad and mom all on the same day?"

"Really?" Robin asked, going pop-eyed.

"You bet."

"Well, I guess I'd say—" his niece let loose with the most unladylike, uninhibited rebel yell "—yee-haw!"

* * * * *

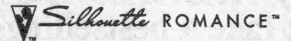
Silhouette ROMANCE™

cordially invites you to the unplanned nuptials
of three unsuspecting hunks and their

SURPRISE
BRIDES

Look for the following specially packaged titles:

March 1997: MISSING: ONE BRIDE by Alice Sharpe, #1212
April 1997: LOOK-ALIKE BRIDE by Laura Anthony, #1220
May 1997: THE SECRET GROOM by Myrna Mackenzie, #1225

Don't miss **Surprise Brides,** an irresistible trio of books about love
and marriage by three talented authors! Found only in—

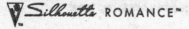
Silhouette ROMANCE™

Take 4 bestselling love stories FREE

Plus get a FREE surprise gift!

As seen on TV!
Free Gift Offer

With a Free Gift proof-of-purchase from any Silhouette® book,
you can receive a beautiful cubic zirconia pendant.

This gorgeous marquise-shaped stone is a genuine cubic
zirconia—accented by an 18" gold tone necklace.

(Approximate retail value $19.95)

Send for yours today…

compliments of ▼ *Silhouette*®

To receive your free gift, a cubic zirconia pendant, send us one original proof-of-
purchase, photocopies not accepted, from the back of any Silhouette Romance™,
Silhouette Desire®, Silhouette Special Edition®, Silhouette Intimate Moments®
or Silhouette Yours Truly™ title available in February, March and April at your favorite
retail outlet, together with the Free Gift Certificate, plus a check or money order for
$1.65 U.S./$2.15 CAN. (do not send cash) to cover postage and handling, payable
to Silhouette Free Gift Offer. We will send you the specified gift. Allow 6 to 8 weeks for
delivery. Offer good until April 30, 1997 or while quantities last. Offer valid in the
U.S. and Canada only.

Free Gift Certificate

Name: _____

Address: _____

City: _____ State/Province: _____ Zip/Postal Code: _____

Mail this certificate, one proof-of-purchase and a check or money order for postage
and handling to: SILHOUETTE FREE GIFT OFFER 1997. In the U.S.: 3010 Walden
Avenue, P.O. Box 9077, Buffalo NY 14269-9077. In Canada: P.O. Box 613, Fort Erie,
Ontario L2Z 5X3.

FREE GIFT OFFER   084-KFD
ONE PROOF-OF-PURCHASE
To collect your fabulous FREE GIFT, a cubic zirconia pendant, you must include this
original proof-of-purchase for each gift with the properly completed Free Gift Certificate.

084-KFD

From the bestselling author of *Scandalous*

Cam Monroe vowed revenge when
Angela Stanhope's family accused him
of a crime he didn't commit.

Fifteen years later he returns from exile, wealthy
and powerful, to demand Angela's hand in marriage.
It is then that the strange "accidents" begin. Are the
Stanhopes trying to remove him from their lives
one last time, or is there a more insidious,
mysterious explanation?

Available this March at your favorite retail outlet.

MIRA The brightest star in women's fiction   MCCI

In the tradition of
Anne Rice comes a
daring, darkly sensual
vampire novel by

As a bonus,
you will also receive
a FREE story by
National Bestselling Author
Stella Cameron,
in the same volume.

MAGGIE SHAYNE

BORN IN TWILIGHT

Rendezvous hails bestselling Maggie Shayne's vampire
romance series, WINGS IN THE NIGHT, as
"powerful...riveting...unique...intensely romantic."

Don't miss it, this March, available
wherever Silhouette books are sold.

Silhouette®

Bundles of Joy

The biggest romantic surprises come in the smallest packages!

January:

HAVING GABRIEL'S BABY by Kristin Morgan (#1199)
After one night of passion Joelle was expecting! The dad-to-be, rancher Gabriel Lafleur, insisted on marriage. But could they find true love as a family?

April:

YOUR BABY OR MINE? by Marie Ferrarella (#1216)
Single daddy Alec Beckett needed help with his infant daughter! When the lovely Marissa Rogers took the job with an infant of her own, Alec realized he wanted this mom-for-hire *permanently*—as part of a real family!

Don't miss these irresistible Bundles of Joy,
coming to you in January and April,
only from

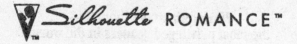

You're About to Become a *Privileged Woman*

Reap the rewards of fabulous free gifts and benefits with proofs-of-purchase from Silhouette and Harlequin books

Pages & Privileges™

It's our way of thanking you for buying our books at your favorite retail stores.

PROOF OF PURCHASE

SR-PP23

Offer expires March 31, 1997

Pages & Privileges ™

Harlequin and Silhouette— the most privileged readers in the world!

For more information about Harlequin and Silhouette's PAGES & PRIVILEGES program call the Pages & Privileges Benefits Desk: 1-503-794-2499

Silhouette®

SR-PP23